PENGUIN BOOKS

HECTOR AND THE SEARCH
FOR LOST TIME

François Lelord has had a successful career as a psychiatrist in France, where he was born, and in the United States, where he did his postdoctorate (UCLA). He is the coauthor of a number of bestselling self-help books and has consulted for companies interested in reducing stress for their employees. He was on a trip to Hong Kong, questioning his personal and professional life, when the Hector character popped into his mind, and he wrote *Hector and the Search for Happiness*, the first novel in the series, not quite knowing what kind of book he was writing. The huge success of *Hector*, first in France, then in Germany and other countries, led him to spend more time writing and traveling, and at the height of the SARS epidemic he found himself in Vietnam, where he practiced psychiatry for a French NGO whose profits go toward heart surgery for poor Vietnamese children. While in Vietnam he also met his future wife, Phuong; today they live in Thailand.

François Lelord's series of novels about Hector's journeys includes *Hector and the Search for Happiness* and *Hector and the Secrets of Love*.

To acces Penguin Readers Guides online,
visit our Web site at www.penguin.com.

Hector and the Search for Lost Time

A NOVEL

François Lelord

PENGUIN BOOKS

PENGUIN BOOKS

Published by the Penguin Group

Penguin Group (USA) Inc., 375 Hudson Street, New York, New York 10014, U.S.A.

Penguin Group (Canada), 90 Eglinton Avenue East, Suite 700, Toronto,
Ontario, Canada M4P 2Y3 (a division of Pearson Penguin Canada Inc.)

Penguin Books Ltd, 80 Strand, London WC2R 0RL, England

Penguin Ireland, 25 St Stephen's Green, Dublin 2, Ireland (a division of Penguin Books Ltd)

Penguin Group (Australia), 250 Camberwell Road, Camberwell,
Victoria 3124, Australia (a division of Pearson Australia Group Pty Ltd)

Penguin Books India Pvt Ltd, 11 Community Centre,
Panchsheel Park, New Delhi – 110 017, India

Penguin Group (NZ), 67 Apollo Drive, Rosedale, Auckland 0632,
New Zealand (a division of Pearson New Zealand Ltd)

Penguin Books (South Africa) (Pty) Ltd, 24 Sturdee Avenue,
Rosebank, Johannesburg 2196, South Africa

Penguin Books Ltd, Registered Offices:
80 Strand, London WC2R 0RL, England

First published in France as *Le Nouveau Voyage d'Hector* by Odile Jacob 2006
Published in Great Britain by Gallic Books 2012
Published in Penguin Books 2012

1 3 5 7 9 10 8 6 4 2

Copyright © Odile Jacob, 2006
English translation copyright © Gallic Books, 2012
All rights reserved

ISBN 978-0-14-312071-1
CIP data available

Contents

Hector and the Search
for Lost Time

HECTOR ISN'T EXACTLY A YOUNG
PSYCHIATRIST ANYMORE

ONCE upon a time, there was a young psychiatrist called Hector.

Actually, Hector wasn't exactly a young psychiatrist any more. Although he wasn't an old psychiatrist yet, either. From a distance, you could still have taken him for a young student, but up close you could see that he was already a real doctor with some experience behind him.

Hector had a great gift as a psychiatrist: when people talked to him, he always looked as if he was thinking very hard about what they'd told him. Because of that, people who came to see him liked him a lot; they felt that he was thinking about their particular situation (which was nearly always true) and that he was going to help them find a way to get better. At the beginning of his career, he would twirl his moustache when he was thinking things over, but now he didn't have a moustache; he'd only grown one when he was just starting out in order to look older. These days, since he wasn't exactly a young psychiatrist any more, there was no point. Time had passed.

But time hadn't made much difference to the furniture in his office. It was the same as when he'd started out. He had an old sofa his mother had given him when he'd moved in, some nice pictures that he liked and a little statue his friend had brought back from the land of the Eskimos – a bear turning into an eagle, which is quite unusual for a psychiatrist's office. From time to time, when Hector felt cooped up after spending too much time in his office listening to people, he would look at the bear with huge wings sprouting from its back and dream that he was flying away too. But not for long, because he would quickly begin to feel guilty if he didn't listen properly to the person sitting in front of him telling him their woes. Because Hector was conscientious.

Most of the time, he saw grown-ups who had decided to come and see a psychiatrist because they were too sad, too worried or just unhappy with their lives. He got them talking, asked them questions and sometimes he also gave them little pills . . . often all three at once, a bit like someone who juggles three balls at the same time. Psychiatry is difficult like that.

But Hector loved his job. First of all because he often felt he was helping people. And secondly because what his patients told him nearly always interested him.

For example, from time to time, he saw a young woman called Sabine who always said things which made him think. When you're a psychiatrist, it's funny but you learn an awful lot just by listening to your patients, whereas they assume you already know nearly everything.

The first time Sabine came to see Hector it was because she was getting upset at work. Sabine worked in an office, and her boss wasn't very nice to her: he often made her cry. Of course, she always cried in private, but, even so, it was terribly hard for her.

Little by little, Hector helped her realise that perhaps she deserved better than a boss who wasn't very nice, and Sabine built up enough self-confidence to find a new job. And these days she was happier.

Over time, Hector had gradually changed the way he worked. At the beginning, he mainly tried to help people to change their outlook. Now, he still did that, of course, but he also helped people to change their lives, to find a new life that would suit them better. Because, to put it another way, if you're a cow, you'll never become a horse, even with a good psychiatrist. It's better to find a nice meadow where people need milk than to try to gallop round a racecourse. And, above all, it's best to avoid entering a bullring, because that's always a disaster.

Sabine would not have been happy being compared to a cow, even though cows are actually kind and gentle animals, Hector had always thought, and very good mothers too. It's true that she was also very clever, and sometimes this didn't make her happy, because, as you might already have noticed, sometimes happiness is not knowing everything.

One day, Sabine said to Hector, 'I think life is just a big con.'

Startled, Hector asked, 'What do you mean?' (That was what he always said when he hadn't been listening properly the first time.)

'Well, you're born, and straight away you have to rush

about, go to school, and then work, have children, and then your parents die and then before you know it you get old and die too.'

'This all takes a bit of time, though, doesn't it?'

'Yes, but it goes by so quickly. Especially when there's no time to stop. Take me, for example, with my work, and evenings with the children and my husband. He's the same, poor thing . . . he never stops either.'

Sabine had a nice husband (she'd also had a nice father, which improves the chances of finding a nice husband straightaway) who worked hard in an office too. And two young children, the eldest of whom had started school.

'I always feel as if I'm up against the clock,' said Sabine. 'In the morning, everything needs to be organised, I have to leave in time to take my eldest to school and then dash to the office. I have meetings I have to be on time for, but while I'm in them the rest of my work piles up, and then I have to rush in the evenings too, pick up my child from school, or get home in time for the nanny, and then dinner, and homework . . . Still, I'm lucky – my husband helps me. We hardly have time to speak to each other in the evening: we're so tired we both just fall asleep.'

Hector knew all this, and perhaps that was partly why he had slowly started to contemplate getting married and having babies.

'I'd like time to slow down,' said Sabine. 'I'd like to have time to enjoy life. I'd like some time for myself, to do whatever I want.'

'What about holidays?' asked Hector.

Sabine smiled.

'You don't have children, do you, Doctor?'

Hector admitted that he did not, not yet.

'Actually,' said Sabine, 'I think that's also why I come to see you. This session is the only point in my week when time stops and my time is completely my own.'

Hector understood precisely what Sabine meant. Especially since he, too, over the course of his day, often felt that he was up against the clock, like all his colleagues. When you're a psychiatrist, you always have to keep an eye on the time, because if you allow your patient to talk to you for too long, the next patient will get impatient and all your appointments will run late that day. (Sometimes, this was very difficult for Hector – for example, when three minutes before the end of a session, just as he'd start to shift in his armchair to signal that time was almost up, the person in front of him would suddenly say, 'Deep down, Doctor, I don't think my mother ever loved me,' and begin to cry.)

Being up against the clock, thought Hector to himself. It was a real problem for so many people, especially for mothers. What could he possibly do to help them?

HECTOR AND THE MAN WHO
LOVED DOGS

HECTOR had another patient called Fernand, a man who was not particularly remarkable, except for the fact that he had no friends. And no wife or girlfriend either. Was it because he had a very monotonous voice or because he looked a little like a heron? Hector didn't know, but he thought it very unfair that Fernand didn't have any friends, since he was kind and said things that were very interesting (although sometimes slightly odd, it has to be said).

One day, out of the blue, Fernand said to Hector, 'Anyway, Doctor, at my age, I've got no more than two and a half dogs left.'

'Sorry?' said Hector.

He remembered that Fernand had a dog (one day, Fernand had brought it with him, a very well-behaved dog that had slept right through their session), but not two, and he couldn't even begin to imagine what half a dog might be.

'Well,' said Fernand, 'some dogs live for fourteen or fifteen years, don't they?'

Hector came to understand then that Fernand was measuring the time he had left in the number of dogs he could have over the rest of his life. As a result, Hector set about measuring the life *he* had left to live in dog lives (that is, which he *probably* had left, for ye know neither the day nor the hour, as somebody who died quite young once said) and he wasn't sure if it would be four or five. Of course, he thought to himself, this figure could change if science made incredible advances that would enable people to live longer, but perhaps on the other hand it wouldn't change, since scientists would no doubt make dogs live longer too, which, you can be sure, no one will ask *their* opinion about.

Hector spoke to his friends about this method of measuring your life in dogs and they were absolutely horrified.

'How awful!'

'Not only that, thinking of your dog dying . . . it's too sad for words.'

'Exactly. That's why I just couldn't have another, because when our little Darius died it was far too upsetting.'

'You really do see some complete loonies!'

'Measuring time in *dogs*?! And why not in cats or parrots?'

'And if he had a cow, would he measure it in cows?'

Listening to all his friends talking about Fernand's idea, it dawned on Hector that what they didn't like at all was that measuring your life in dogs makes it seem shorter. Two, three, four dogs, even five, doesn't make it sound as if you're here for very long!

He understood better why Fernand unnerved people a bit with his way of seeing things. If Fernand had measured his life in canaries or goldfish, would he have had more friends?

In his own lonely and odd little way, Fernand had put his finger on a real problem with time. For that matter, lots of poets had been talking about it for ever, and Sabine had too.

They said . . . the years fly, *time is fleeting*, and time goes by too quickly.

HECTOR AND THE LITTLE BOY WHO
WANTED TO SPEED UP TIME

E VERY so often, children also came to see Hector, and, when they did, of course it was their parents who had decided to send them.

The children who came to see Hector weren't really ill – it was more that their parents found them difficult to understand, or else they were children who were too sad, too scared or too excitable. One day, he talked to a little boy who, funnily enough, was called Hector, just like him. Little Hector was very bored at school, and time seemed to go by too slowly for him. So he didn't listen, and he ended up with bad marks.

Big Hector asked Little Hector, 'Right now, what do you wish for most in the world?'

Little Hector didn't hesitate for a second. 'To become a grown-up straight away!'

Hector was surprised. He had expected Little Hector's answer to be: 'For my parents to get back together', or 'To get better marks at school', or 'To go on a school ski trip with my friends'.

So he asked Little Hector why he wanted to become a grown-up straight away.

'To decide things!' said Little Hector.

If he became a grown-up straight away, explained Little Hector, he could decide for himself what time to go to bed, when to wake up and where he could spend his holidays. He could see the friends he wanted, have fun doing what he wanted and not see grown-ups he didn't want to see (like his father's new girlfriend). He would also have a real job, because going to school wasn't a real job. Besides, you didn't choose to go to school and then you spent hours, days, years watching time passing slowly and getting bored.

Hector thought that Little Hector had let his imagination run away with him about life as a grown-up: after all, grown-ups still had to do things they didn't like doing, and see people they didn't like seeing. But he didn't tell Little Hector that, because he thought that, for the moment, it was a good thing that Little Hector was dreaming of a happy future, since his present was not that happy.

So he asked Little Hector, 'But if you became a grown-up straight away, it would mean that you'd already lived for a good few years, so you'd have fewer left to live. Wouldn't that bother you?'

Little Hector thought it over. 'Okay, it's a bit like a video game when you lose an extra life. It's annoying, but it doesn't stop you having fun.' Then he looked at Hector. 'What about you? Would it bother you to have already lost one or two lives?'

Big Hector thought that Little Hector might become a psychiatrist himself one day.

HECTOR THINKS THINGS OVER

AT the end of each day, Hector thought about all the people he'd listened to who were worried about time.

He thought about Sabine, who wanted to slow time down.

He thought about Fernand, who measured his life in dogs.

He thought about Little Hector, who wanted to speed time up.

And many others . . .

Hector spent more and more time thinking about time.

HECTOR IS CONSCIENTIOUS

HECTOR noticed that, if he asked them, almost all the people he saw had two kinds of worries.

Sometimes, it was the fear that time was passing too quickly, which is quite a distressing fear to have because you can't do much about the speed of time. It's like being on a horse that gallops on without heeding you, which had actually happened to Hector once, and it had given him a real fright.

At other times, it was the feeling that time was passing too slowly, and that . . . well, that's like sitting on a donkey that doesn't want to budge. Of course, it was mostly youngsters who told Hector that, or else very unhappy people who were waiting for things to get better and for whom every day seemed to last for weeks.

Hector thought that in order to help people who were worried about time he could suggest some little exercises to make them think. Because, when you're a psychiatrist, you can obviously just tell people what they need to do to get better, but the chances are they won't listen properly. It's better to help them discover by themselves what would be good for them. Suggesting little exercises to make people think was a method favoured by Hector and quite a few of his colleagues.

Hector took out his notebook and got ready to make some notes. First, he thought of Fernand and wrote:

Time Exercise No. 1: Measure your life in dogs.

This exercise might help people to realise that it was better not to wait too long to do the things you really wanted to do. On the other hand, it could make you even more worried about time passing, and especially about how much of it you had left. Was it such a good exercise then, after all? Hector remembered having learnt at school that some philosophers thought a good life was one which involved thinking every day that one day it would all end. There was even a philosopher who had music played for him every evening at bedtime. Singers would gather at the foot of his bed and sing, 'He lived!', as if it was his funeral. But, as Hector knew, some people are a bit crazy, even some philosophers (and don't tell anyone this, but even some psychiatrists too).

Hector thought of Little Hector.

Time Exercise No. 2: Make a list of what you wanted to do when you were little and dreaming of being grown up.

Again, this could help spur you on to do the things you really wanted to do. But it could just as easily discourage you by making you think it was too late. Hector would have liked to find an exercise which worked for everyone.

Hector thought of Sabine and wrote:

Time Exercise No. 3: Over the course of one day, count how much time you have for yourself. Sleeping doesn't count (unless it's at the office).

It was still very hard to tell what the results of this exercise would be. Some people would realise that they didn't have a moment to themselves and that all their time was spent on other people – he was thinking of Sabine – and others would realise that they had nothing else to do but enjoy themselves or think about themselves. But Hector had already noticed that this didn't always make those people happy. In fact some of them even wanted to kill themselves!

With his three exercises, Hector was well aware that his list was a bit on the short side. Perhaps, if he kept listening to the people who came to see him, it would give him other ideas.

And if that wasn't enough? Well, there would always be time to think about that later.

HECTOR AND THE MAN WHO
WANTED TO TURN BACK TIME

AHA, thought Hector, I feel a new idea coming on. He was listening to Hubert, who was an astronomer. He observed and listened to the stars with such expensive equipment that it took several different countries to pay for it all. Then Hubert and his colleagues did some very complicated calculations to work out how the world had begun a very long time ago. They even wondered what things were like before the world began, and even whether time existed back then.

Hubert had had a complete breakdown the day he realised that, as a result of spending all his time thinking about the stars, he hadn't been paying enough attention to his wife, and she had left him for a man who did nothing much in life, but who was apparently quite funny. Hector was helping Hubert to understand that you shouldn't dwell too much on the past. (It was a bit like the business with the beginning of the world: Hubert was spending all his time trying to understand how this business between his wife and this man had started.) Hector explained to Hubert that knowing whose fault it was wasn't all that important. It would be better for Hubert to look to the future and try to take better care of the next nice woman he met, even if that meant that the next big theory of the beginning of the world was a little delayed.

But Hubert couldn't let it go. 'I wish I could go back in time, back to the time when she still loved me.'

When Hubert said 'to the time when she still loved me', he couldn't stop tears welling up in his eyes. It was terribly sad.

'Now, I'd know how to love her; I'd pay attention; I wouldn't make the same mistakes again. If only I could go back . . .'

And yet, with his very complicated research on stars, Hubert of all people should have known that you can't turn back time – or else it would completely change our understanding of the world and how it works. But, despite this, he didn't stop thinking about it.

'Anyway, Doctor, at our age, you really have to take stock of your life.'

Hector was startled – he thought he was a lot younger than Hubert. He didn't say anything, but afterwards he checked Hubert's date of birth. Sure enough, Hector was younger, but, as it turned out, not by that much.

Hector was a bit disappointed. The only idea Hubert had given him was that he wasn't exactly a young psychiatrist any more, and he already knew that anyway. The only difference was that now he actually felt it, and, as psychiatrists well know, when it comes to knowing and feeling, it's feeling that's important.

In the end, Hubert did give Hector another idea.

Time Exercise No. 4: Think of all the people and things you are not paying enough attention to now, because one day they will be gone and then it will be too late.

HECTOR AND THE LADY WHO WANTED TO STAY YOUNG

THE patient just after Hubert was Marie-Agnès, a rather charming young woman who had a tendency to change boyfriends as soon as they fell in love with her. As a result, Hector had been her psychiatrist longer than she'd been with any of her boyfriends. When you're a psychiatrist, you mustn't fall in love with your patients, even when they are your type. Marie-Agnès had begun to realise that all her friends were married, and that most of the men she was interested in were married too.

'When I think of all the perfectly good men I broke up with when I was younger . . .'

'Perhaps they weren't right for you,' said Hector.

'Oh, but they were. Besides, when I see how they've turned out, I think to myself that I was an absolute idiot not to hold on to them.'

'*All* of them?'

'No, no! Just one.'

'Do you think this might be a useful lesson for the future?'

'The future? But, at my age, I've got much less choice. I think my future will always be worse than my past.'

'If you want to live the same way in the future as you did in the past, maybe,' said Hector.

'Do you mean that at thirty-nine you can't keep living like you did at twenty?'

'What do you think?'

'Ah, but still . . . twenty is the most wonderful time of your life.'

Hector thought that this wasn't true for everyone, but it clearly was for Marie-Agnès.

'Not having a care in the world, being free and able to choose any guy you want, not thinking about the passage of time, feeling that your life is never going to end . . . How I wish I could go back!'

'You were saying a moment ago that you would take the opportunity to choose a good husband quickly,' said Hector.

'Well, there, I'm contradicting myself. Maybe I'd do the same thing all over again.'

'Then why have any regrets?' asked Hector.

'I just miss that feeling that my life will never end . . . because I don't have that feeling any more,' said Marie-Agnès.

Hector had read studies on this. There's a moment when your life seems to stretch out before you like an endless roll of fabric, from which you'll be able to make all sorts of outfits. And then comes the moment when you realise that the roll does have an end, and that you'll have to do some careful calculations if you're going to manage to get even one more set of clothes out of it. (Don't forget, you've known from the beginning that the roll has an end, but, once again, when it comes to knowing and feeling, it's feeling that counts.) Depending on the person, this feeling that the roll has an end hits them somewhere between two and a half dogs and three. Psychiatrists call this a midlife crisis and it puts a lot of work their way.

'By the way, Doctor, could you write me a prescription for my vitamins?'

Hector remembered that, even though Marie-Agnès couldn't slow time down, she tried to slow down its effects on her at least. There were so many things she could try: there were vitamin supplements and supplements of other supplements of every colour imaginable, which she bought on the internet, and workouts three times a week with lots of aerobics. And it's true that, as Hector sometimes noticed, she had a really stunning figure. Then, of course, there were fruit and vegetables at least four times a day (this made Marie-Agnès's mother happy, since she could never get Marie-Agnès to eat her vegetables when she was little), no cigarettes at all any more, not much wine and only good fats (that's to say, none which come from cows or pigs, another reason for not eating those good animals).

Above all, Marie-Agnès avoided sunbathing, because she knew it ages the skin, and she used at least three different sorts of face cream, depending on whether it was morning, night or during the day, and her night cream was called 'anti-ageing'.

Hector thought all this was very good for her health, and would make Marie-Agnès look younger for longer, but it didn't stop time passing.

As it was, Marie-Agnès must have thought the same thing sometimes, because one day she said to Hector, 'When I see myself bouncing up and down in the mirror at the gym or I'm standing in front of all my beauty creams, sometimes I ask myself, what's the point? Why not just finally let go . . . stop caring about all that. Basically, it's a kind of slavery.'

A slave to wanting to stay young. Hector thought that was a very good way of putting it, but he knew that Marie-Agnès would carry on being a slave for quite some time, because the way men looked at her was still very important to her.

When Marie-Agnès had left, Hector looked at himself in the mirror above the mantelpiece just as she had . . . and he noticed, no two ways about it, that for the first time in his life he had a few grey hairs, which you couldn't miss, just above his ears.

So he wasn't exactly a young psychiatrist any more.

In the end, just like all the other times when he had something important on his mind, Hector wanted to talk to his girlfriend Clara about it.

But he took the time to write:

Time Exercise No. 5: Imagine your life as a big roll of fabric, from which you have made all the clothes you have worn since you were little. Imagine the set of clothes you could make with the rest of the roll.

HECTOR LOVES CLARA; CLARA LOVES HECTOR

HECTOR and Clara . . . well, it was a long story, even though they were both still quite young. We'll try to explain it to you, but, as with all love affairs, it's not always easy to understand, even for those involved.

Clara and Hector first met at a big conference for psychiatrists organised by a big company which made medicines and which Clara worked too hard for. Hector had gone up to ask Clara some serious questions about the medicines. Clara had answered him seriously. Then, just after that, Hector had made her laugh; then after that he'd phoned her; then some time after that they'd realised that they were both in love.

And now Clara and Hector were living together.

Clara and Hector sometimes thought about getting married and having a baby, but they hardly ever thought about it at the same time. Sometimes, Hector went off travelling, and when he'd been away, it must be confessed, he'd got up to mischief. And for a while he hadn't really been too sure what he wanted. For her part, Clara had wondered if Hector and she would ever get married. And at times she hadn't really been too sure any more what she wanted either.

But, at this point in their story, Clara and Hector were living together and were starting (once again) to think about getting married and having a baby.

Will they get there eventually? You'll have to keep reading to the end of this book to find out!

One day, Hector talked to Clara about what he'd noticed: that almost nobody was happy with time. And he also told her about this feeling he had, from some of the comments his patients had made, that he wasn't exactly a young psychiatrist any more.

So Clara said to him, 'Oh, you men! You're always a bit slow!'

And she explained to Hector that, for women, the feeling of not exactly being young any more came much earlier than for men.

'How do women notice?' asked Hector.

'The competition appears,' said Clara.

At first, Hector didn't understand what Clara meant, which just goes to show that psychiatrists aren't always that clever after all.

Clara went on: 'And we women are much more aware of the years going by. For a long time, when you're young, you think your life will really get going a bit later, and then one day you realise that this "later" has already been and gone. Usually, this is the point when you begin to see little wrinkles appearing on your face that other people don't notice. Sometimes, I tell myself that if I keep thinking "later", one day I'll realise it's "too late". To have a baby, for example.'

And Clara looked at Hector, and Hector looked at Clara.

All of this showed that, even though Clara seemed to be quite an optimistic girl, there were still times when she thought quite deeply about things. Of course, Hector already knew that, and it was one of the reasons he loved Clara.

Once again, Hector told himself that, even if no one talks about the passage of time, everyone thinks about it.

Apart from babies, perhaps. But, then again, who knows?

HECTOR HAS A DREAM

THE following night, Hector had a dream.

He was in a compartment of a train, just like the ones he remembered from his childhood, with a big corridor and windows you could open with a handle. He himself was a grown-up like the Hector we know now. He was alone and felt a little uneasy. Outside, the countryside rolled by, bathed in late-afternoon sunshine, but it was strange because the countryside was like it used to be when he was a child. You could still see cornflowers and poppies in the fields, big hedges with blackberries and raspberries where birds and rabbits hid, ponds where children fished on their way home from school, their bicycles lying in the grass, and, along country paths, cows and sheep being brought in for the night. Even the sky looked different — it was a softer blue, and the clouds were a purer shade of white. Hector was touched by this sight, and he wanted to share it with someone — perhaps one of his friends was sitting on the train. He went out into the corridor, but there was no one there, and all the other compartments in the carriage were empty.

Feeling a little uneasy, he went through to the next carriage, but there was no one there either. He continued walking up the train, thinking to himself all the while that there had to be *someone* on it.

While he was walking, Hector noticed something odd: the faster he walked up the corridor, the more the train slowed down, and the slower the countryside rolled by. He even had time to catch a glimpse of a pretty farm girl rounding up some nice sheep in the setting sun. If Hector stopped walking altogether to get a better view, the train would speed up, which was a little annoying. So he started running to make the train slow down even more. He ran so fast that eventually the train stopped altogether. But that wasn't such a good thing, since Hector noticed that the landscape outside had become a snowy, icy wilderness, as if the train had arrived at the North Pole. He stopped running so that the train would move off again and get away from this icy and desolate place.

But the train didn't move.

Ice began to creep up all the windows.

Very far away, at the other end of the train, Hector heard a door bang and realised that someone or something had just boarded the train. Footsteps . . . very heavy, very slow . . . were approaching the carriage he was in.

Hector desperately wanted to get off the train, but, the thing was, he couldn't find a door that led outside! He wanted to open one of the windows in the carriage, but all the ones he tried were frozen solid by the ice outside.

In his dream, Hector started wishing he would wake up right away as the footsteps slowly approached his carriage.

Eventually, the train began to move off again, and then went faster and faster, and the nice countryside appeared again. This time, Hector didn't see anyone at all, as if everyone, cows and sheep included, had gone in for the night at the same time as the sun. The only thing he saw was a happy-looking husky bounding along a path.

Hector carried on gazing at the countryside in the setting sun. Suddenly, he wasn't afraid of the footsteps approaching his carriage any more.

The carriage door opened and Hector saw a young monk appear. Now, it wasn't a monk from Hector's country as you might think, but a monk like the ones from China, with a shaved head and wearing a sort of long orange robe which only covered one of his shoulders.

The monk was young, but it was strange because Hector knew that he was actually a very old monk he'd already met in real life. Yet, in his dream, it seemed perfectly normal to him that the monk was very young.

'So,' said the old-monk-who-was-very-young, 'how are things with you?'

Then Hector woke up.

Clara was sleeping beside him. He reached for his notebook and penlight (which meant that he could write without waking anyone up) and wrote down his dream. Hector didn't usually write down his dreams, but he had a feeling that this one was important.

HECTOR GOES TO TALK TO OLD FRANÇOIS

HECTOR wanted to talk to someone about his dream so that he could understand what it meant a bit better. The first person he thought of was Clara, who sometimes had very good ideas, but he knew his dream was a little strange and might have worried her. Besides, since their last conversation, he thought Clara seemed quite sad. From time to time, she looked at herself in the mirror and seemed even sadder.

He'd noticed a very pretty little blue and white jar on the bathroom shelf. On the top, it said 'anti-ageing cream'. He'd told Clara that he thought she was very young to be using anti-ageing cream, but Clara had told him to mind his own business. So perhaps it wasn't a good idea to tell her his dream, because he knew that it was about the passage of time.

Then he thought of an old psychiatrist colleague called François, who was almost as old as his grandfather and always wore a bow tie. Hector thought that François must have listened to lots of people telling him their dreams in his years as a psychiatrist. He would probably have some good ideas about Hector's.

Old François worked in a big room which looked like

an old-fashioned drawing room full of antique furniture and paintings. Even François looked old-fashioned in his bow tie, but Hector knew that he had some quite modern ideas.

So he told him his dream. And he asked him what he made of it.

Old François thought about it. Then he said, 'The problem with dreams is that you never know if it's just the brain jumbling up any old rubbish with snippets of memories to give itself something to do, or if, in fact, it's trying to concoct a story which actually means something.'

Hector was astonished – he remembered that old François had learnt psychiatry at a time when psychiatrists considered dreams to be very important.

Old François saw that Hector was a little disappointed. So he said, 'Of course, at one time, people used to think that a train in a dream symbolised sex . . . wanting to have sexual relations, or being afraid of having them, that sort of thing. But then this idea dates back to a time when having sexual relations was frowned upon in any case. Whereas now it's the opposite . . .'

Old François didn't look as if he had much faith in these old ideas about sexual relations.

'Tell you what,' he said, 'your dream reminds me of what I learnt at school . . . about time. When you're on a train and you throw a ball, someone who's at rest in a meadow sees it travelling much faster than you do, since for him the train's speed is added to the speed of the ball. It's the same with light: if you send a flash of light along a train. But since light always travels at the same speed wherever you see it from, it means that speed . . . no, time . . . is not the same for you . . . no, for him . . . Oh, blast! I can't really remember now. In the end, it all comes down to a question of relativity – you know, Einstein's thing about time being different depending on the speed at which you're travelling.'

Hector vaguely remembered this too. This reminded him of what they say about a teacher and his pupils: the pupils hear half of what the teacher says, they understand half of what they hear, they remember half of what they understand, and they use half of what they remember, which is to say not much, as it turns out. Hector often saw teachers, both men and women, in his office, and often they were sad because they thought they weren't doing any good. Hector tried to get them to change their minds by themselves. So he said to himself that he wouldn't tell them what he and old François had managed to remember about relativity.

But old François went on, 'If you ask me, your dream is about time. Or, to be more precise, about fighting against the passage of time. The train is time, which no one can get away from, or slow down . . . Sadly, we know all too well what's at the end of the line.'

Old François was silent, and Hector got the feeling that he was thinking about it . . . the end of the line.

'And the old-monk-who-was-very-young?' asked Hector, just to stop old François thinking about the end of the line.

'I don't know,' said old François. 'We might say that

he's a reassuring presence for you. But he's someone you've met, isn't he?'

It was true that one day when Hector had gone for a walk just to get away from it all in the beautiful green mountains over in China, he'd stumbled upon a Chinese monastery with a lovely curled rooftop and tiny square windows. That was where the old monk lived, surrounded by other younger monks, all of whom wore an orange robe over one shoulder, and nothing over the other. (It was almost as if they were practising not catching cold!) Hector hit it off straight away with the old monk, who was always in a good mood and could help people understand things without explaining them. The old monk had travelled a lot in his life – he'd even been to Hector's country when he was just a boy, and had done the washing up in a restaurant where Hector still went to have lunch with his father from time to time. From the very first moment they met, Hector and the old monk had enjoyed talking to each other. The old monk had helped Hector understand two or three things about life (without explaining them, of course), and Hector had used this to help his patients. Since then, the old monk and Hector had stayed friends, even if they didn't see each other very often.

Anyway, Hector agreed with old François: his dream did have something to do with time going by. And in his dream he'd tried to stop it, like Marie-Agnès or Clara, but that hadn't turned out very well. Then he'd tried to run away from it by getting off the train, but he couldn't.

Of course, the best thing would have been to go and

tell the old monk his dream, but for a while now, whenever Hector sent him a message over the internet, there had been no reply. He thought that perhaps the old monk had reached the end of the line, and that made him sad.

But he tried not to feel sad, because that in itself was one of the things the old monk had tried to help him understand: feeling sad meant that you hadn't really understood life properly.

HECTOR DISCOVERS A BIG SECRET

IT was around this time that Hector noticed that quite a few of his colleagues didn't have any grey hair at all, even those who were clearly older than him. He wondered if this was a big secret he'd just found out – psychiatrists never get old! But right after making this extraordinary discovery he heard one nurse say to another, 'The new consultant should change hairdressers – it's far too obvious he dyes his hair.' Hector remembered a time when he was a little boy when men who dyed their hair were rather frowned upon. People thought they were men who loved men – at that time, people poked a lot of fun at that sort of love, and pretty nastily at that – or else, irresponsible men who still wanted to whisper sweet nothings at an age when they'd have been better off looking after their family and celebrating the birth of their grandchildren. But Hector said to himself that those days were well and truly over. Nowadays, fine upstanding men, even psychiatrists, and that says it all, dyed their hair to cover up the first snowfalls that had begun to turn their peaks white. (If you like this kind of poetic imagery, we'll try to come up with some more for you.) He knew that these same colleagues also did everything they could to stay looking young, like Marie-Agnès: regular workouts, plenty of fruit and vegetables, watching their weight, and taking supplements and supplements of other supplements. But most of them didn't use face cream yet, at least not any particular type.

On the other hand, old François kept his dazzling white hair just as it was. Hector told him what he had noticed about his colleagues' hair. That meant that even psychiatrists had a problem with the passing of time!

Old François smiled.

'They're still at the fighting stage,' he said. 'I've given up . . .'

And yet Hector knew old François was still interested in love. He'd even bumped into him one night leaving a restaurant with a much younger woman who seemed very lovey-dovey. Hector wondered how old François managed to get women to forget his age and his white hair.

'When I was between forty and fifty,' said old François, 'I appealed to young women who had unresolved issues with their fathers.'

'And now?' said Hector.

'I still do,' said old François. 'They just have to have had an elderly father. Or else a complicated relationship with their grandfather. Of course, there are fewer of those.'

Since old François seemed to be in quite good shape, Hector asked him if this was the secret to his eternal youth.

'No,' said old François. 'Of course, every time a love affair begins, I suddenly feel very young. But every time it ends — obviously, there always comes a time when they finally see me for what I am: an old bloke on medication — then I feel much older . . .'

Hector wanted to ask, 'So why carry on?' Of course, he didn't say that. But old François guessed what he was thinking.

'I'd like to achieve inner peace,' said old François. 'Or think about nothing but my grandchildren. Or have faith, of course. But that grace hasn't been bestowed on me. So now I read philosophy.'

And he showed Hector an enormous library filled with books. Hector recognised some authors' names, like Aristotle, Seneca, Epictetus, St Augustine, Pascal, Heidegger, Bergson, Kierkegaard, Nietzsche, Wittgenstein and quite a few others. (You can copy these down if you like so you won't make any spelling mistakes.)

'And does it help?' asked Hector.

'It passes the time!' old François said, laughing. 'If you like, I'll write a few summaries for you . . . well, my interpretation of them, anyway.'

Hector thought this was a very good idea, because just the thought of reading all those books himself was making him feel a bit tired, and he was sure that old François would have some interesting things to say about philosophers. But, even so, there were some things he wanted to know right away.

'What questions do philosophers generally think about?'

'First of all, they try to define what time is. And it's not easy, because you can't see time and you can't touch it. At the same time, you can't get away from it. "What is time? If no one asks me, I know; if you ask me, I do not know." That's St Augustine.'

'How very true,' said Hector.

'And Pascal, a philosopher who also invented the first mechanical calculator, said that it's useless to define time, since everyone understands it, and if we try to define it we just end up going round and round in circles.'

'I think I'd agree with that,' said Hector.

'But, even so, there is a definition I like . . . "Time is the number of movement with respect to before and after." That's Aristotle.'

'Sorry, what?' said Hector.

He was beginning to find philosophy a bit complicated.

'No, really, it's very simple. You just need to define "number". In fact, Aristotle makes a distinction between what is measuring time, the "numberer" if you will, like the seconds your watch measures (which are all the same) and the thing that's being measured, what happens to you in your life, and Aristotle calls that the "numbered" . . . the seconds of your life. You'd agree that the seconds on your watch, the numberer, are all the same. One second is always the same as the next. But when it comes to the numbered, the seconds of your life – one second of happiness, one second of unhappiness, one second of boredom – they're never the same . . .'

Just then, the telephone on the desk rang. It was his secretary.

'Blast,' said old François, 'I've left a patient waiting in the waiting room!'

When he was leaving old François's office, Hector had several new ideas. He quickly took out his notebook to jot down:

Time Exercise No. 6: Write down everything that makes you feel younger. Then write down everything that makes you feel older.

Hector thought to himself that for old François the answer to both questions was the same: love. Then he also remembered what he'd said about faith: 'That grace hasn't been bestowed on me.' It was strange. Usually, it was the good Lord who bestowed grace. So, it was as if old François thought there was a God who hadn't given him the grace to believe in Him!

Time Exercise No. 7: If you don't believe in the good Lord, imagine you do. If you do believe in Him, imagine you no longer believe. Note how this affects your view of time going by.

Then Hector said to himself that, even if philosophers had trouble defining time, that shouldn't stop others trying, because even if you didn't manage it, it made you think about things.

Time Exercise No. 8: Play a game with some friends. Try to find a definition of time. First prize: a watch.

Hector knew that all these little exercises revolved around one question: is it better to fight against time, to slow it down by trying to act as if you were still young, to act as if time wasn't passing, or rather accept that it is passing, that you can't do anything about it, and that you'd be better off thinking about something else? Or a little of everything all at once? Is it better to live as if you were going to live for ever, or to think that you might die tomorrow, or, at any rate, in the not too distant future?

More and more, Hector felt that if he could find answers to these questions, it would help a lot of people, almost as much as anti-ageing cream and supplements of other supplements.

As always when he'd begun to puzzle over something without finding a solution, Hector had the same impulse: to go on a journey.

That's all very well, said Hector to himself, but where do I start?

HECTOR AND THE OLD MONK

THE next day, in his office, Hector picked up his newspaper to read in peace, because one of his patients had cancelled their session. (When you're a psychiatrist and one of your patients cancels a session, it's a bit like when you're at school and one of your teachers is ill: you get a free period.)

Suddenly, he jumped. What was that picture he'd just seen on the front page of the newspaper? The old monk laughing with his orange robe over his shoulder! Hector was very happy: if there was a story about the old monk on the front page with a photo of him laughing, then he must still be alive! Then he read the story.

The old monk had disappeared, and everyone was arguing.

People from different countries all over the world were accusing China of having made him disappear, because the old monk had already had problems in the past with the people who ruled China. He didn't think like them. As a result, he'd spent quite a long time in rather cold prisons in order to learn how to think in the right way, which is to say, in exactly the same way as the people who ruled China at that time. But, since he hadn't succeeded (he hadn't tried very hard), they'd kept him locked up for many years. But all that was a long time ago and, anyway,

China had changed since then, and the important people in China these days said that if the old monk had disappeared they had nothing to do with it. The other countries said that it was China's fault, and perhaps they had everything to do with it! This had started a big row between all the countries in the world: important people said unkind things to each other in big meetings with microphones, and it was quite funny to look at the picture of the old monk laughing as if he'd just played a great trick on everyone. Of course, straight away, Hector thought of only one thing: finding the old monk. First of all, because he was worried. He wanted to know what had happened to him . . . perhaps the old monk needed some help. And then, because Hector thought that the old monk, with all his wisdom and experience, would be bound to have something very important to tell him about the passage of time. So he sent a message over the internet to one of his friends who also knew the old monk: Édouard.

HECTOR AND ÉDOUARD ARE
GOOD FRIENDS

HECTOR had known Édouard since school, and Hector remembered that, even back then, Édouard had always been in a great rush to do everything. In class, he would finish his schoolwork before anyone else and, since he got good marks, that annoyed the other pupils a little, and sometimes even the teachers, who would say, 'Édouard, stop discouraging your classmates.' Later, Édouard went off to study to become an engineer and build bridges or launch rockets, but, in the end, he didn't become an engineer – he started working in a bank. One day, Hector had asked him why he had chosen this job, because, for Hector, bridges or rockets seemed more interesting.

'I don't want to wait,' Édouard had said. 'Might as well get rich quick. After that, I'll have time to figure out what I want to do.'

Édouard did complicated calculations with money, for example to work out if people should buy pieces of big companies or not. Thanks to his calculations, he made people who were already rich a lot of money, and didn't do too badly out of it himself either. Édouard often changed jobs, because he got bored quite quickly when he stayed too long in the same bank or in the same country. It was a bit like that with his girlfriends. But, once or twice, he'd been very, very badly hurt, because sometimes it's only after you have broken up with someone that you realise that you really love them. But by then it's too late, and the nights are very long, even if you wish away the hours until morning when you can call them. Still, Édouard had found time to get married and have two children, but he'd also got divorced. And now he only saw his children occasionally.

The last time Hector and Édouard had seen each other was in China, the very place where they had both met the old monk. Or, rather, Hector had met the old monk and introduced him to Édouard, because the greatest gift you can give someone is to introduce them to someone new. And Édouard had often gone to visit the old monk in his monastery to talk to him.

After a while, Édouard had even ended up getting bored with money. He'd realised that he was rich enough as it was, and that now he wanted to do something useful for others. He started working for a big organisation which sent people like him to help people all over the world who were quite poor (but not necessarily unhappy). Hector was very glad, because he had a feeling that this new job might finally make Édouard happy. As soon as he'd read the story in the newspaper, he'd sent a message over the internet to Édouard to ask if he had any news about someone they both knew. (Hector was very careful not to say 'old monk' or his name in Chinese, because if his disappearance was that important it was better to be discreet.) Édouard had twigged straight away and had written back:

Come and see me, my friend. We'll be able to talk more easily. Here, time has a different meaning. For the first time in my life, I don't feel as if I'm in a rush any more.

And, besides, some people around here could really do with a good psychiatrist sometimes. Anyway, speak soon.

At the bottom of the message was the name of the place where Édouard was staying. It was so far north on earth that almost all maps stopped just short of it. Well, anyway, it was the land of the Eskimos, or rather, *some* Eskimos, because, in the same way that for American Indians there are Iroquois, Apaches, Hurons, Mohicans, Arapawash and Algonquians (Little Hector knew lots of others besides), so there are several kinds of Eskimo, or rather Inuit, because that's what you're supposed to call them now, ever since well-meaning but rather badly informed people thought, and made everyone else think, that 'Eskimo' was not a nice word.

Hector thought that this would be a lovely trip for him and Clara, and helpful too. Going on a trip would perhaps be good for Clara, who had seemed a little sad lately.

But when Clara saw the place where Édouard was staying on the map Hector had eventually found, she shivered and said no, no way, she didn't want to go and freeze to death up there. Hector was worried, because he'd decided always to travel with Clara from now on to avoid getting up to mischief.

He saw that Clara was looking at him, and then she said with a little smile, 'At least, in cold like that, I don't think there's much chance of you getting up to any mischief!'

But, all the same, Clara's smile was a little sad, and Hector vowed not to get up to mischief ever again.

Will he manage? You'll just have to keep reading . . .

HECTOR AND THE LITTLE BUBBLES

THE last leg of Hector's journey was on the smallest plane he'd ever been on. You couldn't stand upright to go to the toilet and, besides, there were no toilets. Sitting in his seat, he could also see the pilot, or rather the back of a big anorak and a big furry hat. It almost looked as if a bear was flying the plane! What's more, Hector was dressed the same way: he'd bought all his clothes from a list that Édouard had sent him with some rather odd things on it, like silk liner socks and an anorak made out of the same material as the spacesuits of the astronauts who had gone to the moon, and black goggles that looked like the ones you put on when you go to the swimming pool.

Outside, you couldn't see anything, except the pitch-black night and the snowflakes as they landed on the windowpane. Hector was sitting beside the only other passenger: a big American man with huge hands who was coming back to this bitterly cold country to drill little holes very deep down into the ice to find out what the air was like a long, long time ago. Someone else in search of time! thought Hector.

'There are little bubbles of air in the ice,' explained the big American, 'air from hundreds of thousands of years ago.'

He was talking very loudly to make himself heard over

the noise of the engine, and Hector was getting earache from listening to him. Also, he hadn't caught the big American man's name the first time round and he didn't dare ask him again.

'So, what do all these little bubbles tell you?' said Hector.

'That the air was cleaner before!' said the big American, and burst out laughing.

Then he leant over to pull something out of his bag.

'Talking of bubbles . . .' he said.

Hector couldn't believe his eyes when he saw what the big American had pulled out of his bag: a bottle of champagne!

'I brought it for a special occasion,' he explained. 'But, up there, no one knows how to drink it. They like stronger stuff. Better to drink it with you – at least you'll appreciate it!'

Hector had a feeling that he and the big American were going to become very good friends, as soon as he caught his name, that is. The pilot heard the pop of the cork and turned round. This was no bear, but a very pretty woman with ice-blue eyes who looked as if she wouldn't take any nonsense. What's more, she shouted, 'No drinking on my plane!' But the big American showed her the bottle of champagne and held out a plastic cup for her, and then she smiled. She had a very beautiful smile, pure like snow. Hector thought very hard about Clara. Luckily, the pretty pilot only let them pour her half a cup, perhaps just to be polite, and then she turned round to concentrate on flying the plane for the rest of the journey.

Anyway, Hector was glad to have drunk all that champagne before landing, since it wasn't exactly a normal landing: the plane touched down on the ice on runners a bit like skis, and it really was quite bumpy and made a sliding noise, which was a little disconcerting.

'Phew!' said the big American. 'I'll never get used to that.'

Hector had finally learnt the American's name: Hilton. Like the name of a hotel. After a few cups of champagne, he had even jokingly asked Hilton, 'But, Hilton, what happened to your friends Hyatt and Marriott?'

Hilton had only laughed half-heartedly, and afterwards Hector had told himself he was an idiot, because Hilton must have had to listen to a lot of jokes like that from his schooldays onwards.

The door of the plane opened and he remembered that, once, he'd gone to a very hot country. When the door of the plane had opened, it had been a little like opening the oven door to check if the roast is done. Well, here, it was like opening the freezer door or even falling right into the freezer.

Also, it was still dark outside, and all you could see were the lights laid out on the ice, no doubt to guide the plane.

'Hector!' someone called.

Then Hector caught sight of his great friend Édouard, also dressed like a bear, arriving on a snowmobile and waving to him.

Later, sitting behind Édouard as they skimmed along, Hector thought to himself that this was a nice image for time going by: a snowmobile zooming through the Arctic night.

HECTOR IS COLD

THE camp was made up of several very modern tents, and people from different countries lived in them – Hilton and his team of bubble researchers, the pretty pilot when she couldn't set off again straight away in her little plane, and also Édouard.

'Over there, in the distance, that's the Inuit village,' said Édouard.

Hector could make out some faint lights in the dark. The effects of the champagne had begun to wear off and Hector wondered what on earth he was doing in such a cold place, so far from his bed and Clara. Every minute began to seem like an hour to him. Another new experience with time, he thought, but this one was rather painful.

In the not-very-well-lit tent, Hector felt a little better as he listened to Édouard explain things.

'We didn't set up too close to the village so that we wouldn't interfere with their way of life. But, of course, we help them, with medical check-ups for example, and we find ways for them to buy and sell, but at fair prices.'

'But what are you doing here?' asked Hector.

'Once a banker, always a banker,' said Édouard, laughing.

This was Édouard's new job: he had organised a way for the Eskimos to sell furs but at good prices for them. He had also asked his organisation to lend them some money so that they could buy themselves snowmobiles and pay them off little by little.

'In any case, their way of life is going to disappear, just like it has for other tribes. Now they want snowmobiles and modern medicine for themselves and their babies, but with my system it's progressive. They still keep their identity as hunters, they learn how much things cost, they don't get ripped off and they don't end up living on handouts either.'

Édouard explained that, at one time, white people passing through here would agree to trade a knife with the Inuit in exchange for a pile of fox furs as high as the knife standing on its end!

'These poor people were so badly exploited,' said Édouard. 'The only luck they had, compared to the American Indians, is that since no one wanted to settle on their land they were never massacred.'

Édouard poured Hector a little more coffee. Hector thought that Édouard had really changed: before, every time they met, he'd always served Hector wonderful wine.

'It's getting late,' said Édouard. 'Time to go to bed, otherwise you'll be exhausted tomorrow, and, here, the first rule is to keep yourself in good shape.'

Hector realised that he didn't know what time of day it was any more and, looking at his watch, he didn't know if it was midday or midnight.

Édouard explained that this was perfectly normal, what with the time difference between Hector's country and here, and then the journey in the little plane at night.

'All right,' said Hector, 'but what about the old monk?'

'The old monk?!' asked Édouard with a look of surprise.

The old monk hadn't even entered his head when Hector had asked for news of someone they both knew! Édouard had thought that Hector was talking about a nice Chinese girl they had met over in China. Back then, she'd been in quite a bad situation, but Hector and Édouard had managed to get her out of it. And now Édouard could reassure Hector that Ying Li (that was what the nice Chinese girl was called) was still doing well, so much so that she'd just had her second baby with a husband who loved her. She was happy, and what more could you wish for anyone?

Hector was glad to hear the good news about Ying Li, but it wasn't a lot of help to him in finding the old monk. Édouard told him that he also usually exchanged messages with the old monk over the internet, but for a while now the old monk hadn't replied to his messages, which had never happened before. Hector was upset. What if the old monk really was dead after all?

The camp bed was comfortable, but as soon as the lights went out Hector knew he wasn't going to be able to sleep because of the coffee. If he'd known it was night-time, he wouldn't have had it! Édouard was one of those people who could drink coffee without having any trouble sleeping (and who could drink too many bottles of wine without ever getting a headache).

As time began to pass very, very slowly once again, Hector started thinking things over.

HECTOR AND THE PRESENT
WHICH DOESN'T EXIST

A CTUALLY, Hector didn't really think things over – he just let his memories wash over him, and they came back to the surface like bubbles on a big pond filled with champagne, coffee and a kind of sleep which never quite turned into proper sleep. Strangely, it was his years at school which came flooding back to him, probably because minutes had seemed like hours back then too, a bit like they did for Little Hector now. Apart from with some very interesting or funny teachers, Hector had been very bored at school, and he remembered that whenever he looked at his watch, in the hope that at least ten minutes had gone by, only three minutes had, a little like now when he opened one eye to look at the luminous numbers on his watch.

All this proved was that how time felt depended a lot on what was happening to you or what you were doing. If you were doing interesting things, it went by faster. At the same time, Hector remembered that all those hours spent at school seemed like nothing at all in his memory, as if they had taken up a very short space of time, even though they had actually taken many years. On the other hand, thinking back, some holidays seemed to have lasted a very long time, as if he'd spent years playing at the seaside or in the countryside when there were still cornflowers and poppies. That reminded him of a saying he'd heard at school: 'The strenuous life makes hours seem short and memories long.'

All this brought up a big question that Hector remembered as much about as he did about special relativity: does time exist outside us? And what if our whole life was just a dream? But, in that case, who is dreaming and where is he sleeping? And if we were really just someone else's dream, wouldn't that also work the other way round? Did our dreams recount the lives of people who existed somewhere?

By asking himself these sorts of questions, Hector fell asleep and started dreaming (or, rather, reliving a memory in his dream). He was in his office with Madame Irina. Madame Irina was a clairvoyant who had first come to see him because one day she'd realised she could no longer 'see'. Hector didn't quite know what to make of clairvoyance. All he knew was that there was no explanation which fitted with today's scientific thinking, but, after all, only two centuries ago there hadn't been an explanation for where lightning came from or how babies were made either.

So Hector had just helped Madame Irina through the deep depression she had experienced after a man she loved very much had left her. And, after a little while, Madame Irina had begun to 'see' again. And afterwards, like quite a few others, she came back to see Hector from time to time to take stock of things. One day, Hector had asked Madame Irina if she could see the future.

'What does "the future" mean to you?'

Hector thought to himself that Madame Irina was beginning to talk like him.

'Things that haven't happened yet. Tomorrow. Next year. What happens after the present.'

'Doctor, you know very well that the present doesn't exist,' said Madame Irina. 'There's only the past and the future. As soon as you think of the present, it's already in the past. So what I've just told you now is already in the past.'

'And that doesn't exist any longer either,' said Hector, 'because it's in the past.'

'Exactly,' said Madame Irina. 'And, since the future hasn't happened yet, it doesn't exist either.'

Hector thought that if you demonstrated (as he'd just done with Madame Irina) that neither the present, the past nor the future existed, it soon made you wonder whether you yourself existed. It was a little alarming. So he asked a question.

'All right, but what do you "see"? The future?'

Madame Irina thought for a moment.

'I'll be honest with you, Doctor . . . Often, I don't know what I'm seeing. Some images, some feelings, but I don't always know if these relate to my clients' past or their future. That I manage to work out by asking them questions.'

'And are there times when you don't see anything at all?'

'Of course. Seeing isn't something you can do to order. When I don't see anything, I tell my client straight out, and I suggest another appointment. Or else I muddle through,' said Madame Irina, smiling.

'And what do you think is happening when you see the future?'

Madame Irina hesitated. 'Actually, Doctor, I think that future, present, past . . . it depends on the point in time we happen to be in. Just now, we're in the future for the children we used to be, but in the past for the people we will be in ten years. Every moment is at once the past, the present and the future. But we're all stuck on our own little time train, and the countryside always rolls by in the same direction.'

That reminded Hector of his dream about time with the train he couldn't escape from.

'So what are you saying?' said Hector, who was beginning to see where Madame Irina's extraordinary explanation was going.

'I just think, Doctor, that some of us are able to escape our own time train and jump now and again onto other trains which all run to different timetables.'

'That would mean there's more than one flow of time at the same time? Parallel universes?'

'Call it what you want,' said Madame Irina.

And she leant forward to stroke Hector's cheek.

At that point, Hector told himself he really must be dreaming.

But no, it was a tongue licking his cheek, and suddenly he was nose to nose with a big panting husky, and Édouard's voice was saying, 'Noumen! Outside, now!'

Hector woke up completely just as Noumen was getting ready to cock his leg against Hector's bed. Édouard took him outside.

Outside, it was still dark, and Hector wondered if he'd slept for a whole day, but he noticed that there had been *some* change – the sky had gone from pitch black to bluish black, and even to a slightly washed-out inky blue at the horizon. Hector remembered what he'd learnt at school one day when he'd been listening: in this place at the north of all maps, night lasted a very long time.

'We're going to see the Inuit!' said Édouard while Noumen ran in circles around him, barking with joy.

Hector thought to himself that people who lived through a three-month night every winter and a three-month day every summer would surely have some interesting things to say about time.

He took the time to make a note in his notebook, and it was difficult because his fingers were very numb:

Time Exercise No. 9: Take some time to think about things. The past has gone, so it doesn't exist. The future hasn't happened, so it doesn't exist. The present doesn't exist, because, as soon as you talk about it, it's already in the past. So, what does exist?

Seeing this whole landscape at night, Édouard still playing with Noumen, and the lights of the Eskimo village in the distance, Hector thought it seemed as if he was still dreaming.

Time Exercise No. 10: What if your life was just someone else's dream? In that case, where are they sleeping?

HECTOR LEARNS TO SPEAK ESKIMO

HECTOR had expected an igloo made of snow, but they were all sitting in a big stone igloo, which is a little like a house for the Inuit, whereas a snow igloo is more like a tent they put up just for the night.

Hector, Édouard, the village chief and three other younger hunters were all sitting on a very beautiful bearskin rug, and wearing fur themselves. All of this reminded Hector of days gone by, except that it was lit by small electric bulbs which were very modern and used very little power.

'That's the whole problem,' Édouard had told him. 'How do we help them without destroying their way of life? Here, they're the last nomadic Inuit in the area, maybe in the world.'

The Inuit women stayed a little in the background with the children and one or two babies that were being breast-fed, and they looked at Hector and Édouard from time to time and smiled. Some of them were very pretty with their lovely faces framed in fur, but Hector avoided looking their way, because he remembered reading that, for some Eskimos, it was good manners to offer a passing stranger a woman for the night. If that happened, what would become of his resolution not to get up to mischief ever again?

'Jourgoodhel!' said the Inuit chief, raising his glass, or rather his plastic cup.

Hector thought it was an Inuit word, but in fact Édouard had just taught them to say 'Your good health!' And the Inuit had taken to this word straight away.

Hector wondered what they were drinking. It was bitter, sweet and salty all at once, with an aftertaste of rocks, and perhaps a bit of bird too, but not the best bits.

'It's made with the lichen they gather in spring,' said Édouard.

'And is it strong?'

'No, not unless you drink five pints of it.'

Hector saw that the Inuit were looking at him, and he smiled to show that he was really enjoying the lichen beer.

'Drink up,' whispered Édouard.

Hector noticed that everyone else had finished their drink, so he quickly did the same.

The Inuit people smiled again, and straight away they poured him another and said, 'Jourgoodhel!' and Hector understood that they were going to drink those five pints after all.

Time continued to go by very slowly for Hector. He wondered how the Inuit could stand time being so slow, and especially how Édouard, who was always in a rush, coped with it.

'I've got used to it,' said Édouard. 'In fact, this is what it's like during the long night of winter. All they can do is stay in their igloos – they can't hunt, and they live off the reserves they built up in spring. Whole tribes used to die of hunger when their reserves weren't enough to see them through to spring. Now we help them. But if we help them too much they stop hunting and begin living on handouts. Add alcohol, TV, porno films, and then you soon need psychiatrists.'

Édouard explained that elsewhere, further south, there were villages of prefab houses where Inuit people had all the comforts of modern life and almost never hunted any more. The result: a psychiatrist came by every week to work with youngsters who drank, sniffed petrol or got into fights, especially in winter, because now, winter had become boring for them, as had life in general, since they were even more bored at school than Hector when he was little.

'Down there, we took them out of their own time to put them into ours, the white man's time,' said Édouard. 'So no wonder there's trouble.'

Hector suddenly felt that even though the seconds on his watch were the same everywhere in the world, time didn't go by in the same way for people from different parts of the world. The numberer and the numbered, as Aristotle would have put it, and he'd never even seen an Eskimo.

'Then, in winter, everything goes even slower,' said Édouard.

'And what's it like in spring?'

'Well, it's the opposite of now. Everyone's on the go, they hunt, they travel around, they migrate to other settlements, they have parties. And . . . they never stop making love. What's more, women start having periods again, because they don't have any in winter.'

Hector wished he'd come in spring: time would certainly have seemed less slow.

Édouard began to talk to the chief, because, like all the subjects he had taken long ago at school, Édouard had learnt how to speak Inuit quite quickly.

The chief said, 'Oh,' and gave Hector a worried look.

'Damn,' said Édouard, 'I told him you were a psychiatrist, so he thinks you're bringing a curse upon them, like all the other tribes.'

'Tell him I'm on holiday,' said Hector. 'And that I'm interested in time.'

Édouard started talking to the chief again. He listened, looking at Hector the whole time, and then he smiled and said something to Édouard.

'He's asking if you think Inuit time is the same as Kablunak time. Kablunak is their word for us,' said Édouard. 'If our world began at the same time as ours, I mean theirs ... anyway, if the Inuit world got started at the same time as ours,' said Édouard.

No one's told you, but all the while lots of 'Jourgoodhel!' had been going on, and now even Édouard was having a bit of trouble saying what he meant.

Hector replied that, in his country, some people thought that time was the same for everyone, but others (he was thinking of Hubert or Madame Irina) wondered if there weren't different times going on more or less simultaneously.

The chief smiled and spoke to a young hunter who got up and left the igloo. This let in a terrible draught which seemed to Hector to last a very long time.

At the same time, he was watching the little naked Inuit children playing and laughing on the bearskin rug, and he thought that to be a good Inuit you had to start very early.

The young hunter came back with a very old Inuit man dressed from head to toe in Arctic fox fur, and you didn't have to be a great expert in furs to work that out, since his entire outfit was almost covered in fox heads. Hector noticed that the old man could only see out of one eye. The other was pure white, and down that side of his face he had a rather frightening scar. Put it this way, if you'd bumped into him in the middle of the night in your flat on your way to the toilet, you'd have let out a scream that would have woken the whole building.

'I know who he is, but this is the first time I've seen him,' said Édouard. 'You're lucky . . . His eye – a bear did that when he was young.'

The old Inuit looked at Hector with his one eye for a very long time, and Hector also felt all the other Inuit looking at him. Finally, the old Inuit came and sat down in front of him and took Hector's hands in his. Hector thought they felt as icy as . . . but then he tried not to think about it. The old Inuit began to speak to him in Inuit, or at least that's what Hector assumed, because he didn't understand anything. The Inuit carried on looking at Hector, but Hector felt as if it was the pure white eye that was looking at him, and he began to feel sleepy. He told himself he'd drunk too much, and at the same time he felt very light, and then he fell asleep.

At least, that's what he thought.

HECTOR TRAVELS IN TIME

HECTOR was walking on a great snow-covered plain, or perhaps an ice field, he didn't know. All around, there was such an expanse of nothing that on the horizon he almost thought he could see the slight curvature that reminds you the earth is round. As he was walking, he could see himself: his hair had turned as white as old François's and his face was wrinkled too. He wasn't cold, and yet he was dressed as he would be at home, in old trousers, an old shirt, and worn-out shoes that he used to wear a long time ago to go boating. There was total silence – all he could hear was his own breathing and the beating of his heart, which, as it was, he could feel straining a little.

Hector didn't know where he was going, but he really wanted to get off this ice field, because even though he knew it was a dream he was beginning to feel the cold.

Just then, houses began to appear. There were log cabins and, every so often, chalets, which were a little bigger and had fires burning inside. From the doorway of each house, women watched him going by. Hector recognised some of them – ex-girlfriends who stared at him with surprise or, sometimes, a little sadness – and others he had never seen before. There were women of every colour under the sun, and some of them were very, very lovely. Each time

Hector went past one of these houses, he thought about stopping there, telling himself that the woman would welcome him with open arms and warm him up. At the same time, he wanted to keep walking. Perhaps he would find an even more welcoming chalet and an even lovelier lady-friend than the ones before. Thinking of Clara, he had a vague thought that he wasn't supposed to get up to mischief, but she wasn't there and, anyway, cheating in a dream . . . did that still count?

As he was walking, it was getting dark. Little by little, the houses petered out. He wanted to turn back the way he'd come, but he'd gone too far and he could no longer see the houses he'd passed. Besides, with daylight fading over the perfectly flat horizon, he couldn't tell which direction he'd come from any more. Even his tracks had disappeared. He might very well have been going round in circles already. The wind whipped up, darkness was falling, and Hector couldn't go forward or back. Suddenly, he wanted the old monk to appear. That would have made him very happy. But instead it got darker and darker, and Hector only had the noise of the wind and the beating of his rather overworked heart to keep him company in the middle of the plain.

The next thing he knew, Hector was back with the old Inuit, who was speaking to him as he held his hands; Édouard, who was watching them; as well as all the other Inuit, even the babies, who looked a little frightened. Hector saw the whole thing from above, as if he was a bird who could see through the stone and snow of the roof, and then he flew up and away, and everything was dark.

Hector woke up. He was lying in the big stone igloo, and he saw that everyone was asleep, even Édouard, who was lying nearby and snoring quite loudly. There was only one oil lamp burning, which lit the stone ceiling with a gentle orange glow.

Hector began to think about his dream, saying to himself that perhaps it was time he married Clara.

HECTOR DREAMS UP THE WORLD

THE next day (if that word means anything, because, remember, it was always dark), Hector and Édouard came back to their camp for lunch. Inside a big tent, everyone – Hilton, his friends and the pretty pilot – was sitting around a canteen table, and the atmosphere was quite cheerful. It reminded Hector of summer camps when he was a child.

'So, you getting used to it?' Hilton asked him.

'You look very rested,' said the pretty pilot, whose name was Éléonore.

'My friend here met the shaman,' said Édouard.

Éléonore looked very interested.

'Did he show you your future?'

'It scared me.'

He didn't really want to say any more about it. What he'd seen – was that his future? Was he going to grow old all alone on an endless plain, or could his future still be changed?

'In any case, you can't predict the future,' said Hilton.

'Oh yeah?' said Éléonore. 'What about the weather forecast? That wouldn't be predicting the future, now, would it?'

Hilton admitted that you could perhaps predict what

the weather would be like one or two days in advance, but not people's lives.

'And why not?' said Éléonore. 'It's just more complicated: there are more factors at work.'

'In my old job,' said Édouard, 'we would try to predict stock-market prices. It was just as complicated as the weather.'

'It's simply that, in order to predict people's lives, you'd need even more data than you would to predict a storm coming,' said Éléonore. 'But in theory it's not impossible. The future is always determined by the present. The problem is that we don't know all of the present well enough to predict all of the future.'

What Éléonore said reminded Hector of a word he'd heard at school one day when he wasn't bored: 'determinism'. He remembered that a philosopher with a nice wig had said that if someone knew absolutely all of the conditions of the past and present, they could predict the future exactly. Yet another question to ask old François . . .

'There are some people who think you can find out your future from a horoscope!' said Hilton. 'That's always made me laugh.'

'And what if there was some truth in it?' said Éléonore, looking quite annoyed.

'Pah!' said Hilton. 'Thinking that people can predict the future using astronomical data from ancient times . . .'

'It's easy to dismiss what you don't understand,' said Éléonore.

Hector guessed that Éléonore read her horoscope. She flew a plane in dangerous conditions, taking into account the weather forecast and the position of the stars calculated in an entirely scientific way, but she still checked her horoscope beforehand. Like Clara, for that matter. It fact, it was the first thing she looked at when she bought a women's magazine. And Clara could do some very complicated calculations on her little computer. Surprising, isn't it?

'Anyway,' said Hilton, 'you can interpret horoscopes any way you want – it's the opposite of science.'

'Not at all. It depends which ones you read.'

Hector wanted to stop a conversation he could tell was going to end badly, because he could see that it was really secretly about something else, as all conversations that end badly always are. He had a feeling that Hilton had been in love with Éléonore and she'd wanted none of it, and that now Hilton liked to annoy her a little, because she had snubbed him. Or else he wanted to show that he was a real man, and not the obedient little lapdog that he'd sometimes been before.

'The future's already happened,' said Hector.

Everyone sitting at the long table looked at him. He hadn't realised that he'd spoken so loudly. He tried to explain himself better.

'What you call the future, it's already in the past, somewhere else, in another time.'

Everyone kept looking at him without saying anything. Hector felt a little embarrassed. He tried to make up for it by saying something funnier.

'The life we're living, here, now, might be someone else's dream. And this dream might depend on what that person had for dinner before going to bed . . . A good day for you is thanks to that person having some nice vegetable soup and sole with boiled potatoes for dinner, and having sweet dreams; a bad day is down to too much sauerkraut and white wine before going to bed.'

'Let's get some fresh air,' said Édouard.

Once they got outside, Édouard gave Hector a worried look.

'You feeling all right?' he asked Hector.

Hector said he felt perfectly fine, and then, all of a sudden . . . he passed out.

HECTOR SINGS IN THE SNOW

T HEY went back to the Inuit camp by snowmobile. Édouard thought that Hector might have drunk too much lichen beer the day before, that he wasn't used to it, and that the Inuit might have a cure. Hector let himself be talked into it, but he was a little worried: what if the cure was worse than the ailment?

While the wind from the ride was starting to freeze a little bit of his cheek left exposed between the edge of his goggles and his scarf, Hector noticed a change in the landscape: there was a band of clear sky on the horizon, as if the sun was about to come up.

Hector noticed the Inuit near their igloo: they were on their knees facing the glow of light on the horizon. Édouard turned off the snowmobile so as not to make any noise.

'They've started praying,' he said.

It was the time of year when the Inuit prayed every day that the sun would finally appear.

'They have an advantage over us,' said Édouard. 'They only expect out of life the best of what it's already given them . . . like spring. At least, they were like that until they met the white man. Now they want snowmobiles and, soon, TVs.'

An old Eskimo noticed them and came to meet them. As he got closer, Hector recognised the shaman, but he seemed much smaller than the day before, and he was simply dressed in bearskins, like the others.

Édouard began talking to him in Eskimo. The shaman replied, smiling.

'He says that you're a great traveller, for a Kablunak,' said Édouard. 'He says he can take you travelling again.'

'Ask him if he took me into my future.'

Édouard started to translate again.

'He says he doesn't know. Maybe into one of your past lives or one of your future lives – he can't tell.'

This answer reminded Hector of what Madame Irina had said to him about her clients, and he thought that she, too, was a bit of a shaman.

'He thinks I have many lives?'

'For them, time is cyclical,' said Édouard. 'Everything comes around again like the seasons, like the sun disappearing, then coming back. We die, like the sun, and then we come back.'

Hector thought to himself that if he went travelling again with the shaman he wouldn't really like to find out all the mischief he'd got up to in his past lives - only the bits he could avoid repeating in his future lives.

'And how do they measure time?' asked Hector.

'Nowadays, some of them have watches.'

'Yes, but before?'

'They had a sense of time, and they'd also watch the sky changing. Here you have to get back to camp before nightfall.'

Hector remembered having read in a journal for psychiatrists that most people were able to judge time without a watch without being too far off, except when they were asleep, and sometimes even then. But, with watches and clocks everywhere you looked, everyone had got out of the habit.

He resolved to write:

Time Exercise No. 11: Hide your watch. From time to time, make a note of what time you think it is. Then compare it with the time on your watch.

The old shaman listened to Hector and Édouard talking to each other, and he didn't look as if he was getting impatient. All of a sudden, Hector thought of all the people he had met in his country who were pressed for time. Up against the clock.

'Can you ask him if they are ever in a rush?'

'It's a bit difficult to translate,' said Édouard.

He started talking to the shaman again, who thought it over a little before he answered.

'He says that sometimes they are pressed for time, yes.'

'But when?'

The shaman began to sing in such a deep voice that it sounded like rocks rubbing against other rocks.

Édouard listened and began to translate, trying to sing it the same way.

'The wind is getting up; we have to build an igloo fast . . . Nanook the bear is running on the snow; we have to chase after him and urge our dogs on . . . the ice floe is beginning to crack, and we have to get across it fast on our sled . . . My sweetheart is back at the village; I have to go home before she chooses another hunter . . .'

The chief started singing his song again, but this time with a little laugh. Édouard laughed too.

'The Kablunak-who-counts-fast is coming back to the camp; we must count our pelts. And become the Inuit-who-go-fast . . .'

Hector thought to himself that, before, Eskimos were never rushed by anybody else! They just had to go faster from time to time to catch the daylight which was running out, animals that were being hunted or their sweetheart who was distant. Then, even if you messed up and found yourself one night with your sled on an ice floe which was cracking, it wasn't so bad, since your life would begin again. This was the kind of time all men had lived by for a very long time, in fact almost ever since men and women had existed.

All of a sudden, Hector wanted to sing, and it came to him out of the blue. So, with his feet in the snow, he sang:

Chase, chase the snow,
Chase the daylight,
Or chase your sweetheart,
Chase after bears,
Chase the ice,
But don't chase time,
No, never spend too much time
Chasing the white man's time.

HECTOR HAS A TICKET

'I don't think you should stay around here for too long,' said Édouard.

'But why? I'm really enjoying myself. And, also, Inuit time is very interesting.'

'That's as may be, but I think you're becoming . . . strange.'

'No, it's just that I've loosened up a little,' said Hector, even though he was clinging on to the seat of the snowmobile for dear life because they had just gone over a very big bump.

Far behind them, all the Inuit as one started singing a new song, and it was Hector's song with Inuit words, thanks to Édouard's translation. As they were leaving, the shaman had given Hector a bear tooth.

'If we stay, they're going to offer you a woman,' Édouard had said.

So they'd left on their snowmobile, and Hector was delighted that he hadn't got up to any mischief this time. He thought that he deserved a pat on the back, since he'd noticed how much the Inuit women had appreciated his talents (undiscovered until then) as a singer-songwriter. During the very long nights of winter, it's always nice to have a singer at home for entertainment.

They arrived at the foot of a glacier that they could make out quite clearly because, on the horizon, it was almost daylight, even though the sun hadn't appeared yet. The rest of the night sky had turned light blue. (A glacier is like an enormous ice cream that somebody has dropped, which is beginning to run very slowly while staying frozen.) For some years, this glacier had hardly been moving forward at all, and, instead, it had just melted a little every summer. Perhaps that was why Hilton and his team of bubble hunters had set up their equipment on it: they had to make the most of the glacier while it was still there.

Éléonore was there too, and Hector noticed her little red plane sitting a little further away on the ice. Édouard stopped the snowmobile near a big three-legged drilling machine which was going to look for bubbles very deep in the ice. Some warmly wrapped-up people were operating it, while Hilton and Éléonore were talking a little further away. They looked glad to see Hector and Édouard coming.

'Feeling better?' Éléonore asked Hector.

'Never felt better,' said Hector.

Hilton asked Édouard if he thought that the Inuit might help them move his equipment to another pocket of bubbles.

'No problem,' said Édouard. 'They like the idea of going back in time thanks to the little bubbles in the ice. In fact, it's like their way of life: managing to do a lot with very little.'

Hector remembered that before the arrival of the first

white men's boats, the Inuit had never seen wood. They made their sleds out of bone and the hides of animals they hunted. And they used the fat of the animals to make fires.

Hector asked Hilton and Éléonore if they would be staying long in this part of the world.

'I love flying,' said Éléonore, 'and here's no worse than anywhere else. Actually, no, it is worse than other places, but that's what makes it interesting. And the scenery is so wonderful in spring.'

Hector asked Éléonore where she usually lived. She said that she left her things in a hotel room in the last white town before you reached Inuit country.

Hector realised then that Éléonore had neither a man nor a home in her life. She seemed to have nothing to tie her down, just like when she flew off over the ice field. He wondered if she thought about time passing (Hector had noticed the little wrinkles Clara had talked about at the corners of Éléonore's eyes) and about the time she had left to have a baby.

'In fact, living this life,' said Éléonore, 'makes you forget that you're a grown-up. You forget that time is passing.'

Saying this, she smiled and glanced over at her little red plane, which, from a distance, looked like a pretty toy sitting on the ice.

'You might forget it,' said Hilton, 'but we are grown-ups, and time *is* going by, faster and faster.'

And, again, Hector could guess what this conversation was actually secretly about.

'A very long time from now,' said Éléonore, 'I too might be a mass of little bubbles in the ice, because one day I'll crash my plane. And people like you will be trying to find out what was in the blood of a twenty-first-century woman.'

She let out a charming little giggle. Hector thought that he had already met young women who were quite difficult to tie down, but Éléonore couldn't have been far off the world record, as he could see from Hilton's miserable expression.

'Anyway,' Éléonore said, turning to Hector, 'a shrink like you would say that charging headlong into the future is a way of running away from something! I know all about these kinds of things . . .'

She looked as if she was gently making fun of what psychiatrists say.

'The problem,' said Hector, 'is not being able to run away from wanting to run away from time, which is running away from you.'

'Running away from wanting to run away from time, which is running away from you?' asked Éléonore.

'Yes, always wanting to run away from time is like a prison. The bars are invisible, but we carry them with us.'

He thought about his dream, about his fellow psychiatrists' hair, about Marie-Agnès and her supplements of other supplements, about Clara and her anti-ageing cream, about François's love affairs, and then also about Éléonore who didn't want to live like a grown-up.

'Of course,' Hector continued, 'getting out of this

prison may be even more difficult than flying over the ice field at night in a blizzard.'

Éléonore looked at Hector, Hector looked at Éléonore, and Hector thought to himself that Édouard was right . . . the lichen beer made him say things he would have kept to himself before.

And he also thought that he'd better not stay around here for too long . . .

HECTOR AND THE PRESENTISTS

HECTOR was drinking very hot coffee and reading old François's reply on Édouard's computer.

My dear friend,

The funny thing about reading philosophy is that you realise we are all philosophers without knowing it.

Anyway, the philosopher who thought that we could predict the future if we knew all of the past and present was Laplace, an astronomer living at the time of the French Revolution who knew that we could predict the motion of the planets. Since he realised that we would never be able to know all of the past and present, he thought that to predict the future we'd have to get around this with probability calculations. So he invented them, these calculations – there's even a law of probability named after him. I'm talking about a time when some philosophers were also very good at maths.

The past which doesn't exist because it doesn't exist any longer, ditto for the future because it doesn't exist yet, and the present which doesn't exist because straight away it's in the past – you'll find all that in St Augustine! According to him, time only exists within us, because at every moment we perceive the past, the present and the future in what he called 'an extension of the mind'.

The business of parallel universes makes me think of another big debate in philosophy. Some think that the past, present and future are really not the same thing. We remember the past, we imagine the future, etc. We live in the present in a three-dimensional world, and that world only exists in the present.

Others say that the past, present, future, it all comes to the same thing. It just depends on the point in time you happen to be in. Every object has three dimensions, as well as a fourth: time.

In fact, the first lot are called eternalists, the second presentists. Your clairvoyant patient is a presentist!

But I'm going to stop there, since I realise that up at the North Pole you must be very cold, and you shouldn't stay still for too long.

HECTOR AND THE HALF-EMPTY GLASSES

HECTOR took off his gloves and opened his little notebook. He thought about Inuit time, and time in his childhood in the countryside. It gave him an idea:

Time Exercise No. 12: Thinking about your past, try to predict your future (at least, your most probable future).

He thought to himself that this was an exercise that you sometimes did for other people: predicting whether their marriage would last, whether they'd be successful in their job or whether their children would be happy. But you almost never did this exercise for yourself! He too would have liked to predict the future and find out where all of these exercises were going to take him. More than anything, he hoped that he would find the old monk and show him his list.

'Right, that's us, the engine's warmed up!'

It was Édouard coming to tell him that the plane was ready to take off. They said goodbye and promised that they would see each other again soon.

Hector found himself on the plane with Éléonore and an Inuit mother who was taking her baby to see a doctor down south, because the baby wasn't putting on any weight, even though she was feeding a lot. Despite the noise of the engine, the baby was very quiet, and was feeding away with a very intent look on her face.

So as not to disturb them, Hector sat beside Éléonore. She was very busy looking at quite a lot of gauges of every colour, and pushing and pulling even more little levers. Then off they went, sliding faster and faster along the ice, and suddenly the engine made a terrible high-pitched noise like the howl of a mortally wounded animal, and then they were up in the air, climbing higher and higher.

The baby had kept sucking away after she'd closed her eyes, and her Inuit mother was watching her anxiously. Hector thought that an old Englishman's idea had been proved right yet again: no matter what colour someone's skin was, or what part of the world they lived in, the same feelings made them laugh, cry or worry. In the old bearded Englishman's time, his idea hadn't gone down very well with people in his country, because they were the sort who thought they were much better than everyone else, especially when it came to people of a different colour. And then the old Englishman, even though he was a very nice man, had annoyed them even more by announcing that all men (and women too, don't forget) were descended from apes, including people who drank tea with their little finger sticking out while saying 'Hmm'.

Hector also hoped that the baby wasn't too ill.

'So,' said Éléonore, 'did you like it?'

'Yes,' said Hector. 'It's like time travel. They live a little like we did a very long time ago.'

'Not for much longer,' said Éléonore.

'Yes, because of us.'

'That's true,' said Éléonore. 'On the other hand, now their babies can get proper medical care. Before, a lot of them died.'

Hector thought that that was at least one good thing you could say about the civilisation he and Éléonore came from: babies had a better chance, and so did the women giving birth. On the whole, people nowadays lived a lot longer than the Inuit did in the old days.

'Mind you,' said Éléonore, 'when you see what we do with our extra time, you wonder if it's a good thing. Old people's homes? Not for me, thanks.'

Hector remembered that this was another of his great civilisation's new inventions: old people's homes. Were they really something to be proud of?

Hector thought to himself that, what with landing and taking off on the ice and flying through blizzards all the time, Éléonore stood quite a good chance of avoiding an old people's home.

On the other hand, by not being in a hurry to have lots of babies who would later become nice children who would look after her when she was old, as they did in all the other civilisations in the world, Éléonore ran a greater risk of landing up in the 'Forget-Me-Not' room with someone saying to her: 'Now, dear, would we like some stewed prunes today?' This person wouldn't necessarily see in Éléonore the young woman she had once been.

That gave him an idea for old people's homes, and for

all elderly patients in hospital: they should always have some photos of themselves when they were young up on the wall in their room, so that people could properly understand who they really were. Because, even though the past didn't exist any longer, remembering it was still helpful in understanding someone. Hector wrote:

Time Exercise No. 13: Whenever you meet an elderly person, always imagine what they were like when they were young.

After a thought like that, Hector felt a little sad, and suddenly he really wanted a glass of champagne.

'And what about you? What are you going to do with the time you have left?' asked Éléonore.

Well, thought Hector, the future only exists in the present, when we live it or when we talk about it.

He thought of different answers, and then he plucked up his courage and said, 'Maybe have a baby with the woman I love.'

Éléonore was quiet for a while. Then she said, 'Actually, I don't think I'm optimistic enough to have a baby, I think that life is too difficult, that the world might be worse in the future, and I don't want to bring a child into this world if it's going to have a life of suffering . . .'

This was another glass-half-full or glass-half-empty way of seeing life, thought Hector. He also said to himself that, for her to think that way, Éléonore must have already had quite a lot of half-empty glasses thrown in her face when she was a little girl.

HECTOR UNDERSTANDS THE
PSYCHIATRISTS' SECRET

HECTOR found his town the way he had left it, with its inhabitants who had a lot more things than the Inuit, but who worried a lot more than the Inuit about their future and about time going by.

Hector was still troubled by the idea that the old monk might be dead and that he would never see him again, and he regretted not having gone to see him more often.

To take his mind off it, he asked Clara about hair dye for men. In her opinion, was it good or bad?

'I don't like it,' said Clara. 'But on the other hand, if it's done well, it's true that it can make a man look younger. And to find a job these days it's best not to look your age too much. You're lucky that you're your own boss. In your line of work, it's the opposite, since grey hair makes it seem as if you're wise and experienced.'

'All right,' said Hector, 'but then why do some of my colleagues . . . ?'

'It's not for their patients, if you ask me,' said Clara. 'It's to appeal to people younger than them. If I ever catch you dyeing your hair, I'll break the bottle over your head!'

This remark made Hector happy, because it meant that Clara thought they would still be together when he had lots of grey hair! He remembered his dream of walking on the ice field with hair as white as old François's. Perhaps the old Inuit had taken him travelling to one of his past lives.

To take his mind off things, Hector turned on his computer and checked to see if he had any messages.

And, yes, Édouard had sent him a message.

Dear Hector,

I have something quite difficult to tell you.

The Inuit shaman talks about you every day now. For him, you're the Kablunak-who-travels. Here's what he said to me yesterday.

The Kablunak-who-travels must go to the top of the mountain. He must find the not-Kablunak-but-not-Inuit-either-who-laughs-often. Otherwise, very bad lives for him and for someone he loves, later on.

What do you make of that?

Édouard

CLARA AND THE TICK-TOCK
OF TIME

WHEN Hector told Clara that he wanted to go and
see if the old monk was still in his monastery on
top of the mountain over in China, and that they could
both go there together, Clara looked uncomfortable.

'I'd like to, but I'm tired,' said Clara. 'And if I take my
holidays now it'll be hell when I get back.'

Here's me trying hard not to get up to mischief,
thought Hector, and I'm really not getting any help!

But he saw that Clara didn't seem worried that he was
going all by himself. Perhaps because she could tell that
he didn't want to get up to mischief any more. Perhaps
also because she thought that if he was going to see an old
monk in a monastery he wouldn't be in the mood to get up
to any mischief. Which just goes to show that women are
sometimes a little too optimistic.

Mind you, you have to be to decide to have children
and look after them for years. That shows how wonderful
nature is (but not always very nice, all the same).

In fact, Hector thought that Clara didn't look worried,
but sad.

'Are you sad because I'm leaving?'

'Yes . . . no . . . ' said Clara.

'Yes-no or no-yes?' asked Hector with a very serious face, and he managed to make Clara laugh. But even her laugh was sad.

'So?' asked Hector.

In the end, Clara said that they loved each other, she was sure of that now, but she wondered whether they would ever get round to getting married and having a baby.

'I feel as though the time for doing it without thinking too much about it has been and gone,' said Clara.

Hector was a little taken aback, but Clara explained that she felt that the life of a relationship between two people was a bit like the life of a person.

'You see, I think that a couple starting out together is like a child. At first, everything seems fresh and new; then it grows up, understands things better and becomes a grown-up; then it becomes middle-aged, then elderly and then an old person. The couple dies because one of the pair dies, or, more often nowadays, because they split up. I think a couple is like a human being which is born, grows old and then dies.'

'And you don't think ours is alive any more?'

'No,' said Clara, 'that would be too easy. But I do think getting married and having a baby is easier when the couple is very young, and when they still don't know each other that well. If they live together without deciding anything, the couple gets older and, after, it's harder to make the effort to change. There's no longer the enthusiasm there was at the start.'

'So you don't want to have a baby?'

With that, Clara began to cry.

'I don't think I'm at my best just now,' she said, sniffing. 'At the moment, I feel time's ticking away, that my life will be over soon . . . that I haven't done anything very interesting. Am I even interesting?'

Little warning lights went off in Hector's head: *negative view of the past, pessimism, low self-esteem.* Every psychiatrist in the world knows that these ways of seeing things are signs that you might be deeply depressed. And Hector also remembered how sad Clara had been lately, even when she put on her anti-ageing cream before going to bed.

He took her in his arms. She let him, and continued to sob on his shoulder. Hector was filled with tenderness, and he was kicking himself for not having noticed before that Clara might have been depressed for quite a while.

But we all know that cobblers' children have no shoes, and Hector had some colleagues who had only noticed there was a problem at home the night their daughter had swallowed a bottle of sleeping pills, or their wife had tried to hang herself with the curtains. When you're a psychiatrist and you come home, it's as if you take off your psychiatrist goggles and turn back into someone who's not that much more observant than average . . . and, what's more, since you've listened and talked to people non-stop all day, sometimes you're so tired that you don't even want to listen to the people you love, and that can make them unhappy.

Hector thought that Clara needed to go as soon as possible to see a psychiatrist he trusted – old François – because he would be able to tell if she was depressed or just feeling a little blue.

Meanwhile, he heard Clara sniffling on his shoulder, saying that she felt that time had gone by too quickly, that everything seemed to be over, and Hector wondered what was worse: not noticing time, or seeing it going by everywhere you looked.

HECTOR AND THE KINGDOM
OF HEAVEN

THE day before he left for China, Hector saw some patients in his office that he wanted to see before he went away.

He wanted to know whether they were doing well enough to cope with not seeing him for a while or whether he should quickly send them to one of his colleagues, or even send them to have a rest in a quiet place with very nice men and women in white coats.

First, there was Roger.

Roger was a big strapping fellow who looked as if he could be difficult, but really he was quite harmless. The problem was that, for almost all his life, Roger had believed that God (and sometimes the devil) spoke to him personally. He even heard voices in his head, and he often answered out loud, and this surprised the people he came across in the street. Roger wasn't a bad soul at all, but he could quickly fly off the handle when people made fun of him or, even worse, the good Lord. As a result, he'd spent quite a lot of time in a psychiatric hospital on enough medicine every day to knock out a horse, or several ponies, if you prefer.

But, for some years, Hector had managed to get

Roger to keep his thoughts to himself, telling Roger that he could only talk about them with him and other people he liked. Roger was doing much better, or, at any rate, he was taking less medicine and didn't really need to go into hospital any more.

'So, you're going away?' said Roger.

'Yes, but not for very long. Two or three weeks at the most.'

'You never know,' said Roger.

'You never know what?' asked Hector.

'Ye know neither the day nor the hour . . . We are in the hands of the Almighty . . .'

Hector was a little worried, because when Roger got started like this it could go on for a long time, and he had lots of other people to see that afternoon. He had an idea.

'Tell me, Roger, what do you think about time passing?'

Roger frowned, which was quite unnerving, but Hector knew that it was because he was thinking things over. Finally, he said, 'Time doesn't pass . . . we do.'

Hector thought that was a very good answer.

'I read it,' said Roger. 'Or I heard it . . .'

Hector could see that Roger was beginning to listen to the voices in his head. So he asked him, 'And knowing that we pass on, that we grow old, how does that make you feel?'

'It brings us closer to the Kingdom of Heaven,' said Roger. 'Then time will end and eternity will begin!'

Roger looked very happy thinking about the Kingdom of Heaven.

'So you're not afraid of growing old? You don't want to slow time down?'

Roger looked a little shocked by the idea of wanting to slow time down.

'But time belongs to God alone!' he said.

Hector said to himself that Roger might not have been all there, as they say, but on the other hand, he seemed a lot happier with time than most of the people Hector knew. If only Roger could have talked about all of this more calmly, thought Hector.

Later, he wrote in his notebook:

Time Exercise No. 14: Imagine that growing old will bring you closer to the Kingdom of Heaven (or the place in your religion).

Of course, some people might think that it brought them closer to hell, but they weren't usually the people who would truly deserve it.

HECTOR IS A DOG PSYCHIATRIST

HECTOR'S secretary told him that someone had asked for an emergency appointment.

It was Fernand with his dog.

'I have a problem,' explained Fernand. 'When I leave him at home on his own, he howls, he wees everywhere and he chews the legs of the sofa.'

He was such a calm and well-behaved dog that, to look at him, it seemed impossible to imagine him behaving so badly.

'Do you think it's to punish me for going out?' asked Fernand.

'No,' said Hector. 'It's because when you go away and he's left all on his own, he has no way of knowing that it's not for good. It's a panic response.'

Now, Hector might seem awfully clever to have understood Fernand's dog so quickly, but it's because he had met vets who specialised in dog psychology, and the more these people studied dogs, the more they found that they were like people or children.

'Your dog can't imagine the future,' said Hector. 'He only lives in the present, or in the very immediate future.'

'That's true,' said Fernand. 'When he hears me filling his bowl, he knows he's going to get fed. Or when I go and get his lead, he wags his tail because he knows we're going to go out.'

'There you go,' said Hector. 'That's the very immediate future. But he doesn't think into the future. He lives in an eternal present.'

Fernand looked at his dog. Then he said, 'At least *he* doesn't measure his life in dogs . . .'

Hector prescribed a medicine for anxiety in people to Fernand's dog. In fact, it was a medicine for depression, because actually that's a bit how being abandoned feels. So the medicine also worked for abandonment anxiety.

Afterwards, this session got Hector thinking. Animals didn't live in the future or the past. This saved them a lot of worrying, like thinking about how long their life would last. On the other hand, when the present was going badly, none of these fine animals could make it better with hopes of a brighter future or good memories of a happy past. The hell of the present seemed eternal, without beginning or end.

If we gave people the freedom to choose, would they rather live like animals? For that matter, all those people who said that you should always live in the moment, without worrying about the future or chewing over the past, weren't they advising people to think like cows? And yet some of them called themselves philosophers, which, in case you've forgotten, means 'those who love wisdom'.

The wisdom of cows? The carefree life of cows? Their Being-cows-in-the-world, as a philosopher with a little moustache would have put it, who was so difficult to understand that even people who wrote books about him didn't agree on what he'd meant. More questions for old François.

Hector wrote down:

Time Exercise No. 15: Imagine you are a cow. You don't remember that you were little. You don't know that you're going to die. Would you be happy? If you could choose, would you rather be a cow? Or maybe another animal? Which kind?

Hector remembered that another philosopher, this time one with an enormous moustache, had actually written that cows were very lucky to live in an eternal present without being burdened with memories. He thought that the only way to be truly strong or happy in life was to be capable of forgetting! What was strange and terrible was that later this philosopher died of an illness which took away his memory, and even the thoughts inside his head!

Hector was thinking about what kind of animal he'd like to be. A seagull? A dolphin? But his secretary told him that Marie-Agnès was waiting in the waiting room.

HECTOR AND LOST TIME

'I'VE found someone even crazier than me!' announced Marie-Agnès.

'Crazier than you?'

'Yep, definitely!'

And Marie-Agnès gave a little laugh which showed her very nice sparkling white teeth (she had them cleaned very often). She explained that she had found quite an important man who was madly in love with her.

It was rather good news.

'He's nearly twenty years older than me,' said Marie-Agnès.

'Oh really?' said Hector.

'Oh, he doesn't look it at all! And for me that's not a problem.'

'So, what is the problem?'

Marie-Agnès had brought a photocopy of the man's diary with her. All the pages were very full, with things like 'Parliament' or 'Arrive in Munich' or 'Executive Committee'. Then, at the bottom of each day, there was a little note. Hector read: *Time lost: 35 minutes. Time left: 7,456 days.*

'The thirty-five minutes, that's the time he reckons

he's wasted that day. A good day for him is when he manages to make it less than ten minutes.'

'And the 7,456 days?'

'That's the number of days he thinks he has left to live.'

Marie-Agnès explained that the man – he was called Paul – had done some calculations: you could work out how much time you *probably* had left from the age your relatives were when they died, your blood pressure and some other things doctors know.

So Paul had come up with his own time exercises! Every day he was aware that his Being-in-the-world, as the philosopher with the little moustache would have put it, was soon going to end – in a word, that one day he was going to die. Hector would very much have liked to meet Paul to see if this thought really helped him.

'I really wanted him to come with me to see you today and for us to talk together, but he didn't have time!'

In any case, Hector didn't have a lot of time either because he had to go to China. Going to China? you may ask. And leaving Clara all by herself when she was already so sad? Actually, he'd been thinking about delaying his journey for a while and waiting until she was better before he went. But when he'd told Clara that he was going to put his trip back a little, she'd said no, absolutely not, and that he had to go to China straight away, otherwise she would feel it was her fault if he didn't find the old monk.

'But still . . .' said Hector.

Just then, Clara had a very good, and very clever, idea. (You can see why Hector loved her so much.) She told

Hector that the old monk might be able to explain about time going by, and when Hector came back he could tell her and that might help her a lot. And that also reminded Hector about what the Inuit shaman had said.

So Hector left for China, thinking a lot about Clara.

HECTOR GETS SOME PERSPECTIVE

ON the plane, there was a little screen on the cabin wall, and Hector was able to read:

Current time at point of departure: 16:00
Current time at destination: 23:00
Time remaining: 11 hours
Estimated time of arrival: 10:00

This reminded him of a very strange thing that mankind had only understood very late on: the time of day isn't the same in different places in the world, because the earth is round and it spins round just in front of the sun, a little like a plumpish ballerina spinning in front of a wood fire. Midday is when you're right in front of the sun, and so the different people in the world have to take it in turns, just as the ballerina can't warm both sides of her body at the same time.

In the toilet, Hector had an idea (he often had ideas in the toilet) – if there hadn't been a clock on the plane, would he have been able to measure the passage of time? He could have worked it out from the time the air hostess served breakfast, lunch and dinner, or tried to see what the different landscapes the plane flew over looked like.

But what if he'd been all by himself on the plane and all the blinds had been down, if he hadn't been able to see anything moving inside or outside the plane, or if he'd locked himself in this toilet? Hector could have worked out the time by counting his heartbeats, but again that would have been because something was moving. And what if he'd been tied up and unable to take his own pulse, as doctors do? Even so, he would have been aware of time passing, by being aware of the thoughts running through his head. But, then again, that would have been because something was moving. It was actually tiny molecules firing in his brain. He told himself that he'd had a good think about things. He left the toilet, went back to his seat, took out his little notebook and wrote:

Time Exercise No. 16: Concentrate and be aware that there's no time without movement, and no movement without time. Time is a measure of movement.

Hector reread what he'd written, but all of a sudden he couldn't really understand what he'd meant any more. The thought had already moved on inside his head and wasn't very clear now.

Suddenly, he remembered what old François had said: 'Time is the number of movement with respect to before and after. Aristotle.' He had to read Aristotle, or rather reread him, because he remembered having read bits and pieces of him at school. He began to think things over again, but not for long because it was time for breakfast and the air hostess put a tray down in front of him with lots of nice food on it.

Well, not *that* nice, because this time Hector was travelling in the cheapest part of the plane, and his knees were beginning to complain. He thought to himself that time was going to pass very slowly for him, a little like the night he'd spent in Édouard's tent. But, wait! . . . He'd spend the time thinking about Clara and about all the things he could do when he got back to make her happier.

HECTOR TALKS TO HIS NEIGHBOUR

ON the plane, Hector was sitting beside a Chinese man with little round glasses who was reading a newspaper in Chinese. He was a very polite man – the first time his elbow had brushed against Hector's, he'd taken it off the armrest straight away, and since Hector was quite polite too, he'd done the same thing, and now they were both keeping their elbows tucked into their sides, and the armrest between them remained empty. The Chinese man looked quite old, but Hector noticed he'd dyed his hair. So the fear-of-time-passing disease was indeed what doctors called a pandemic, which meant that it had spread all over the world. And they wouldn't invent a vaccine for that overnight, thought Hector with a sigh.

The air hostess came and asked him if he'd like prawns with noodles, or duck with vegetables. Hector chose the prawns, because he thought he would have been able to kill the prawns himself (you just had to take them out of the water), but definitely not a duck that is able to feel fear, joy and sadness, much like us. They can even follow you around like a little dog if you get one very early when it's just hatched, whereas with prawns you'll always be disappointed.

The air hostess was pretty, but she looked a little

grumpy, as if she'd had enough of her job and of asking people dozens of times: 'Prawns or duck?' Once again, Hector counted himself very lucky to have a job which was different every day. Because if 'the strenuous life makes time seem short and years long', on the other hand, the more you do a job that's always the same, the more chance you have of getting bored, and the years will go by faster. He hoped that the air hostess would get a promotion, or that she would find a nice husband, or else a new job that would seem more exciting, at least at first.

Hector also thought that he could take her mind off it by starting a conversation with her, but then he remembered Clara crying on his shoulder and he didn't want to any more. This just proved yet again that even if the past doesn't exist any longer, it leaves traces – so it still exists a little in the present. And inside Hector some traces bore Clara's name.

He glanced at the man's newspaper in Chinese and what did he see? You've guessed it – another photo of the old monk laughing! But it was strange, because there was also another photo of him dressed as a monk, but it looked as if it had been taken a very long time ago, and he was surrounded by Chinese men and women dressed as in the olden days – a little like the people you see in *The Blue Lotus*, Hector's favourite Tintin adventure.

And yet, in the photo, the old monk looked almost as old as he was now. Must be a photo of his father, thought Hector.

He asked the Chinese man very politely what the

article said about the old monk, and the man answered in fairly good English that he'd disappeared.

Hector said that he knew that already, that it had been in the newspapers in his country for a few days now, along with the big row between China and the other countries who said it was China's fault that the old monk had disappeared.

'Yes,' said the Chinese man, 'but there has been a new development.'

He explained that for a long time everyone had thought the old monk was the son of another famous old monk, and then people realised that, no, the old monk wasn't the son of the other old monk, but he *was* him, his father, or rather not his father since he didn't have a son. To put it more clearly, it was the same old monk the whole time, not a father and his son. And as soon as people started to realise this and talk about it the old monk had disappeared.

'And what age would that make him now?' asked Hector.

'A hundred and twenty, a hundred and thirty years old,' said the Chinese man, looking at Hector through his little round glasses with a smile that was almost apologetic for saying such strange things to a Westerner.

Hector understood why the old monk was so wise: he'd really had time to understand things properly.

HECTOR AND THE SONG OF TIME

Hector was back in the Chinese city at the foot of the mountain by the sea. Once again, he noticed the smell of the sea, the huge towers gleaming like razor blades – some new ones had sprung up since he'd last been there – and, of course, the mountain he had gone up one day on a little train, and where, as he'd walked up even higher, he had stumbled upon the old monk's monastery.

His hotel wasn't the same one as last time. He had done this on purpose, because he didn't want his room to bring back too many memories – like the nice Chinese girl, Ying Li, singing to herself in the bathroom in the morning. As a result, Hector felt a little lonely, because now his friend Édouard wasn't in this city any more, but was with the Inuit, the old monk had disappeared, and he wondered if it was a good idea to call the only other person he knew in this city, who was, of course, Ying Li.

He went out into the street and found himself in the middle of lots of Chinese men and women, nearly all dressed as if they were going to the office because it was early in the morning, and, also, it was a part of China where people worked a lot in offices and not at all in the fields. All these people looked as if they were in a great rush, and Hector came very close to being jostled on the pavements where everyone was a little tightly packed together. No doubt about it, even though the people here might look a bit like the Inuit (after all, they were distant cousins), they had completely switched over to white man's time, and now they too were up against the clock. On the other hand, it meant they earned a lot more money than the other Chinese people in China, and they were able to afford better apartments and to send their children to school for longer. This would later on allow these dear children, in turn, to earn more money, and so on . . . It seemed going back to Inuit time was truly impossible. Besides, even the Inuit wanted to leave it behind.

At the foot of the huge towers, Hector found the tiny station again and the wooden carriages of the little train which went all the way up to the top of the mountain. There was still an old Chinese man in a cap who was selling tickets, and he smiled at Hector as if he recognised him. Hector waited on the little train until it was due to leave. When the time came, there was still no one else on board, but then two tourists appeared, and they came and sat down opposite him.

They were old people who came from a country not far from Hector's which still had a queen, and this Chinese city had belonged to her for quite a few years. They both had white hair like old François, their eyes were pale blue and they moved rather slowly like old people do, but they were smiling and seemed very happy. They said a friendly hello to Hector when they sat down opposite him.

Hector was glad to see people who still looked so

happy to be alive and loving each other after what was probably many years spent together, and who probably had barely one dog left to live, as Fernand would have put it. Perhaps they would give him some good ideas for time exercises that could help others. Because the problem with psychiatry is that you mostly study people who aren't doing so well, whereas if you spent a little more time studying people who are doing very well, it might give you some good ideas to help the ones who are not.

On the other hand, Hector knew that there were also people who had a knack for being happy, and who didn't have much to say about it, a little like someone who sings every note perfectly, but can't explain how they do it.

The train began to move off slowly with a grinding noise, because it was suspended by cables, a little like a lift. The slope would have been too steep for a normal train.

Little by little, the train climbed up past the tops of the buildings and came out into the forest, which looked like a jungle, and it was strange to find such a wild forest so close to such a civilised city.

The train came out of the forest and the view was magnificent – you could see the sea in the distance, looking leaden in some places and sparkling in others where the sun was breaking through the clouds, then there were islands, other distant mountains, and mainland China.

The old couple were pointing these wonders out to each other and saying 'How beautiful' or 'Look at this, darling', as if they wanted to make sure the other didn't miss anything.

Hector asked them if it was their first time here. And the old man said no; after they'd retired, they'd gone home, but they'd lived in this city for many years before that, when it still belonged to their country, in fact. They liked coming back here every year, and each time they found the scenery just as wonderful.

Trevor and Katharine – those were their names – had both been teachers. Katharine had taught drawing, and Trevor, great writers and poets. Some of their pupils had fond memories of them and still sent them greeting cards every year.

'We'd happily have stayed here,' said Katharine, 'but we wanted to see more of our children and our grandchildren.'

'And, anyway, it's not the same,' said Trevor, 'even if it is still wonderful.'

'How is it not the same?' Hector asked.

'The city has changed . . .' said Trevor.

'I think you'll find it's *us* who've changed, darling!' said Katharine.

And this made both of them laugh, even though it wasn't such a happy thought really. It struck Hector how perfectly these two sang the song of time.

HECTOR MAKES SOME FRIENDS

TREVOR and Katharine carried on talking to Hector. When the train reached the top, they all got off together and started walking along the road in the beautiful Chinese mountains. Hector was careful to walk very slowly so as not to tire them out. Talking to them, he realised that they had known the old monk too!

'He was very famous here,' said Trevor. 'When he came back after all those years over there . . .'

And Trevor pointed towards mainland China off on the horizon, where nothing but fun things happened to monks at one time.

'We went up to the monastery and had tea with him,' said Katharine. 'I wanted to have him round to our house, but he apologised and said that he'd rather we came to see him at the monastery, that at his age he didn't want to go into town any more, that everything went too fast for him. He said that in his monastery he could forget that things had changed so much.'

Hmm, thought Hector, could the old monk also have had problems with time?

'And his age?' asked Hector.

'Ah, that whole business . . .' said Trevor.

'Anyway, if it's true,' said Katharine, 'we're still not old enough to have known him when he was young!'

And they both gave another delightful little laugh.

The monastery came into view, with its lovely curled rooftop and tiny square windows.

But it wasn't peaceful like last time, because there were cars parked outside, quite a few people who looked as if they were waiting to get into the monastery, and even news vans from different television stations. And also some police officers in uniform stationed in front of the door to the monastery, to stop too many people trying to get in and coming to bother the monks.

Near a television van, a Chinese woman was standing in front of a camera, speaking into a microphone. Her English was as perfect as Katharine's, and her hair hardly moved in the wind.

'The monks' representative has reiterated that he has no comment,' she said.

Hector saw a big television screen in the van behind her, and on it he could see her on one half of the screen, while on the other half there was a calm-looking presenter with grey hair sitting in a studio which must have been very far away. The presenter asked the woman, whom he called Jennifer, if there had been any more news on the old monk. Jennifer said, 'No, John,' but she pointed out that she was actually right outside the monastery where the old monk had lived until he disappeared. Then John reminded the viewers that they, he and Jennifer, were talking to them live, and that Jennifer was actually right outside the old monk's monastery. And Jennifer said that was right, she was there, and that everyone was wondering what had become of the old monk. And they carried on talking like that long distance without really saying anything. But since the old monk's disappearance and his supposed age was a big story they had to talk to each other every hour for quite a long time, and Hector thought that this must be quite difficult and boring for them, a little like asking 'duck or prawns?' hundreds of times. Time must have passed very slowly for them, because if duration is 'the uninterrupted upsurge of novelty', as a philosopher Hector vaguely remembered once said, there wasn't much novelty for Jennifer and for the people watching her all over the world. Television went from one place in the world to another very fast – not far off the speed of light – and all that to make time pass very slowly for the people watching it!

Hector had an idea. He was pretty sure that the old monk wasn't in his monastery any more, because somebody would have been bound to find him in there, including the Chinese police, who had good reason to find him so that everyone would stop bothering China. On the other hand, people watched television almost everywhere in the world – in the world's great hotels, but also in huts or in tents everywhere else. And he'd just hit upon a way of giving the old monk a sort of signal.

He apologised to Trevor and Katharine, and, while Jennifer was still valiantly talking without really saying anything, he went to explain to the young Chinese men on her team that he had known the old monk well, because he was a psychiatrist specialising in time and he had often been to visit him, since the old monk really knew his stuff when it came to time.

HECTOR IS ON TV

AND that's how Hector came to be on television for three minutes nearly everywhere in the world, with the beautiful green Chinese mountains he loved so much in the background. He explained that nowadays everyone seemed more and more worried about time going by and was asking themselves questions. And he thought the old monk was bound to have answers to these questions.

'Can you give an example?'

'Is it better to fight against time by trying to stay young for as long as possible, or accept that time is passing and accept your age?' said Hector.

Jennifer managed to stay calm and collected, but Hector could tell that his question had given her a bit of a shock. He was kicking himself for not having been more tactful – perhaps it was another effect of the lichen beer. He'd just noticed at the corners of Jennifer's eyes the famous little wrinkles that Clara had talked about. She must have been starting to get worried when she was on TV, thinking about the competition appearing, and about all the pretty young things who wanted her job (whereas the presenter with the grey hair wouldn't be worried at all). It's really very unfair: a few wrinkles on men don't scare women, and some even like them, whereas men don't feel the same way about wrinkles on women at all. This was one of the things that made Hector doubt just how wonderful nature really was. Some people thought that everything natural was perfect.

Jennifer thanked Hector very much, and on the screen he saw that John looked happy too. It was almost as if, as well as 'duck or prawns', he'd let them put another dish on the menu: 'Duck, prawns or seafood risotto?'

'Well done, you were great,' said Trevor.

'Oh yes!' said Katharine. 'You know, we've never really asked ourselves that question: is it better to fight against time . . . ?'

Trevor and Katharine sang the song of time perfectly. And yet they had never wondered about it. Hector was determined to understand why.

HECTOR SINGS ON TOP OF THE MOUNTAIN

TREVOR, Katharine and Hector met up again in a little café not far from the top of the mountain. Hector was very happy because he was sure they would teach him something about the passage of time. He was careful, though, not to ask them questions which were too direct, like, 'And how does it make you feel having no more than a dog, or even half a dog, left to live?'

In any case, he didn't need to ask any questions, because Trevor and Katharine wanted to share their experiences with Hector, whom they had taken to straight away.

'Actually,' said Trevor, 'Katharine and I don't see things in the same way. She has faith, but I haven't.'

'And to think that after forty-six years of marriage he hasn't changed!' said Katharine.

Hector thought back to all the people he'd met who truly believed in the good Lord. He'd noticed that this helped a lot of them cope with growing old and even dying, since if you believed in the good Lord then you believed that the world you were born into wasn't the most important, but that there was another more important one after (and perhaps before, for that matter).

Trevor, on the other hand, managed to cope with growing old without believing in the good Lord. Hector really wanted to know how he did it.

'Well now,' said Trevor, 'in order to cope with time passing, you need luck – and a little philosophy.'

'Luck?' asked Hector.

He could hardly see himself saying to his patients: 'All you need is a bit of luck and then everything will get better!'

'Yes,' said Trevor, 'to be lucky enough to stop wanting to do things at the same time as you stop being able to do them. For instance, I loved playing tennis . . .'

'He was a great player,' said Katharine, 'and it even annoyed me a little, because all the women in the club would hang around him.'

'But,' said Trevor, 'with the tiredness and the pains in my knees, I stopped wanting to play. I'm happy with my memories, but I have no regrets. And I feel that, in my life, everything has always turned out pretty much like that – you stop wanting to and you don't regret anything.'

Trevor said that when the end came he hoped he'd have the same luck: to be tired of life when it was time for his to stop.

'Of course,' he said, 'it also helps to be fairly happy with the life you've lived.'

'And also to see your children happy,' said Katharine.

'That's also luck,' said Trevor.

'That's going too far – surely we've got something to do with it if our children are happy!'

'That's true,' said Trevor, 'especially you, my love.'

Trevor said that he hadn't read that much philosophy, but one saying had stayed with him and helped him a lot in his life: 'Do your best to change the things that can be changed, accept the things that cannot be changed and know the difference between them.'

Trevor explained that it was supposed to be a Roman emperor who had come up with this, because, as well as being a general who won battles, he was a philosopher. Hector thought this was such a wonderful saying that he resolved to use it in one of his little exercises.

'And also reading poetry,' said Katharine.

'Oh yes, that's true,' said Trevor. 'Listen.

> *'Time passes swift, my love, ah! swift it flies!*
> *Yet no – Time passes not, but we – we pass,*
> *And soon shall lie outstretched beneath a stone.*
> *And for this love we talk of – Death replies*
> *Forever not one word of it, alas! . . .*
> *Then love me, while thou art fair, ere we are gone!'*

And as he said the final line, Trevor took Katharine's hand and kissed it.

She seemed very moved, so Hector took over, softly singing:

> *'When it's time to sing of cherry season,*
> *And cheerful nightingales and mocking blackbirds*
> *Will all celebrate,*

Beautiful girls will lose their reason,
And lovers will have hearts full of sun,
But how short it is, the cherry season,
When you go in twos, to pick as you're dreaming
Of pairs of drop earrings . . .
Cherries of love, of the same bud
Fall 'neath the leaves in drops of blood . . .
But how short it is, the cherry season,
Coral-pink earrings you pick as you're dreaming! . . .'

Katharine and Trevor clapped, and then Katharine began to sing in a suddenly very young voice:

'As time goes by . . .
It's still the same old story
A fight for love and glory
A case of do or die.
The world will always welcome lovers
As time goes by.
Oh yes, the world will always welcome lovers
As time goes by . . .'

This time, it was Trevor who seemed moved.

Later, on the way back on the little train, Hector wrote:

Time Exercise No. 17: Put together a collection of
beautiful poems about time going by. Learn them by

heart and recite them to friends who are older and younger than you.

But he hadn't forgotten Trevor and the Roman general's philosophy.

Time Exercise No. 18: Do you spend time trying to change the things that can be changed? Do you try to accept the things that can't? Do you know the difference between them? Make sure you can answer 'yes' to these three questions.

In any case, thought Hector, if ever there was one thing you couldn't change, it was the passing of time. So, best not to think about it too often!

HECTOR AND TIME REGAINED

Now, all of this had kept Hector busy, but he knew perfectly well that he was going to end up calling the nice Chinese girl he had met a long time ago, Ying Li.

They had only spent two evenings and two nights together, and then life had taken them in different directions, but Hector still felt moved when he remembered Ying Li. He remembered she had been a little intimidated on the first night when he'd asked her to dinner, but so happy singing to herself in the bathroom in the morning, then so sad crying in his arms in a taxi at night.

He decided to arrange to meet her in a café which was on the top floor of one of the city's museums. That way he thought it wouldn't bring back too many memories for either of them since they'd always met at night, in the kind of places where people only go very late in the evening.

Hector and Ying Li had had what they call an impossible love, but that didn't mean it hadn't left Hector with some lasting memories, and perhaps Ying Li too, he thought. Still, he knew she was married to a nice boy from the same country as Hector, and that she'd just had her second baby. Édouard was the godfather to the first. And Hector, of course, loved Clara! So it was an even more impossible love than at the beginning, since Hector and Ying Li were both happy.

But when he saw her appear in the big café where he was waiting, he went weak at the knees.

From a distance, she was exactly the same Ying Li as he remembered, just as beautiful and dainty and charming. When she smiled at him, he saw that she seemed moved. As she sat down, she lowered her eyes shyly exactly like the first time and her cheeks were all pink, and Hector could feel that his were too.

Then Hector saw that time hadn't stood still for Ying Li either, that she had filled out a little, and that those famous wrinkles had begun to appear if you really looked for them. Ying Li must have seen his first few grey hairs and his own little wrinkles.

Hector wanted to tell Ying Li that she was still as beautiful as ever, because he thought so, but, at the same time, he told himself that perhaps this wasn't something you said to a married woman. But in the end he said it anyway, and he saw it made Ying Li happy, especially as she must have already seen in his eyes that he thought she was still as beautiful as ever, despite the time that had passed, which just goes to show that Hector still felt love for Ying Li and not just desire for her fleeting beauty.

Then they began to talk.

But what did they say to each other? Very simple things, which people who still love each other say, even if both of them also love another person who loves them back, and both are going to stay with that other person. They caught up with each other's lives. Hector wanted to know how Ying Li's baby was, and she was very well (because it was a little girl).

Ying Li wanted to know if Hector had married Clara, and he said soon, probably. And Ying Li smiled again and told him that was what she wished for him, because, after all, happiness was getting married and having children, as she now knew, and she would have liked Hector to know that too. Hector asked after her son, who must have been nearly six by now, Hector reckoned. As it happened, Ying Li said that he was visiting the museum downstairs with one of Ying Li's sisters and they were going to come up and see them.

And indeed a young lady who looked quite like Ying Li, but less stunning, was coming towards them holding a little boy by the hand.

The little boy looked a little bit Chinese, but not entirely, and this was to be expected since his father was from the same country as Hector. Hector remembered that he was called Eduardo, after his godfather, Édouard.

Ying Li told Eduardo to say hello to Hector, and the little boy looked at him with surprise as he shook his hand.

'You're already a big little boy,' said Hector, who thought Eduardo was very big for his age.

Eduardo looked as if he was thinking about this, then he said, 'Could you also say that I'm already a little big boy?'

'Yes, you could,' said Hector. 'And soon you'll be a big boy, full stop.'

'I don't know if I'll like that,' said Eduardo.

'Why not?'

'Because, after, I'll soon be a man, and then one day an old man, like Grandpa.'

Little Eduardo didn't think like Little Hector at all! He'd rather have slowed time down. Hector knew that this meant he was very happy with his mummy and daddy, and that he wanted it to last for ever.

Ying Li said that Eduardo was always asking questions and thought about things a lot, but that he was almost always happy. Ying Li's sister just smiled because she didn't speak any English at all.

Hector and Ying Li carried on talking to each other for a while. Ying Li had also gone to see the old monk with Édouard, but, since then, she hadn't heard anything either. Hector told her that he was going to try to find him. Ying Li said that she would like it if Hector called her again if he was staying a little while longer in the city, or the next time he came back. Hector said yes, of course, but at the same time he thought it was better if he and Ying Li didn't see each other too often, and he knew that, in her heart of hearts, Ying Li thought that too.

Then they said goodbye, and Little Eduardo shook Hector's hand again and said, 'Goodbye, Mr Hector.' And Hector watched the three of them walk away, and Ying Li gave him a last smile and a little wave, and Hector was alone.

He ordered a glass of red wine, he thought about things for a bit and then he took out his little notebook and wrote:

Time Exercise No. 19: Meet the children of the women you ~~love~~ *loved when you were younger.*

HECTOR AND THE MAN WHO
LOOKED AT THE STARS

HECTOR thought that perhaps he would go home, because there was no sign of the old monk, and there wasn't much point in waiting around for him. Then he remembered that Hubert, the man who looked at the stars, was staying somewhere around here . . . that's to say, if you kept going towards the Chinese mountains, you'd come across higher and higher ones, and at the top of one of them was a huge telescope which was so expensive that it took several countries to buy it, a little like when all the children club together to get their mother a present for Mother's Day.

From the city he was in, you could go straight to almost anywhere in the world. Hector found himself back on a plane with Chinese characters written on it, where this time the air hostess offered him rice with prawns or noodles with duck, but also some kind of steamed buns. There weren't many people on the plane because, in the region where he was going, the birds had a tendency to catch a rather nasty cold, and so tourists preferred to go to other places in the world where there were diseases which were much more dangerous to people, but which Jennifer didn't talk about on the television every day.

The airport he landed at was very basic: it only had one runway and a concrete building that reminded him of the ones they built when he was little. The wind was fierce, and all the men and women who looked Chinese were wearing fur hats; Hector promised himself he'd buy one.

He was very glad to see Hubert arriving in a car that also reminded him of his childhood.

'It's nice to have a visitor,' said Hubert. 'Only seeing colleagues gets tedious after a while.'

And Hector understood what Hubert meant, because it was the same for him; after two days at a psychiatric conference, all he wanted to do was leave. Even if, individually, he liked some of his colleagues, as a group, they were a little like an enormous plate of pasta that you can't finish.

You might be wondering if it was all right for a psychiatrist to visit his patient outside the office. Certainly, that's debatable. But Hector wasn't seeing Hubert for the kind of therapy which lasts for years, where the psychiatrist has to stay very quiet and mysterious. Instead, Hector was helping Hubert get through a difficult time. It was more like the relationship between an ordinary doctor and his patient. So it wasn't going to be a problem down the line that Hector had come to see Hubert.

The car got out of town quite quickly. It was easy as the city wasn't very big and there weren't many people on the roads either because of the cold and the wind. They started going uphill, up a little road. The countryside was beautiful, but Hector was having trouble appreciating it because, from time to time, they would meet lorries as big as houses tearing down the road in the opposite direction without seeming to take much notice of Hubert's car. Every so often, at the bottom of a ravine, Hector caught sight of the wreckage of a lorry with its wheels in the air.

'You get used to it,' said Hubert. 'Here, people don't have the same sense of danger as back home.'

He explained that a very long time ago the ancestors of the people driving the lorries had conquered half the world on their little hairy horses. So it was quite natural that their descendants would be rather fearless. Finally, they arrived at the bottom of a cable car, and then there they were, in a little cabin that was swinging around a bit too much for Hector's liking.

'The telescope gobbled up so much funding,' said Hubert, 'that they were a little short of money for the cable car.'

Hector said to himself that people imagined that astronomers led very quiet lives watching the stars. In fact, being an astronomer could be almost as dangerous as being an astronaut, except you fell from less high up, but still high enough to hurt yourself really badly. At the top, it reminded Hector of Éléonore and Hilton's camp: little prefab buildings, and then, in a kind of very large bubble, the huge telescope which looked at the sky through an enormous slot. And lots of antennas around it, like very big TV satellite dishes that were there to listen to the murmuring of the stars.

'You came at the right time,' said Hubert. 'Last week, it was hell – we were running late!'

Hector looked into the distance at the vast landscape of mountaintops and the infinite sky above them, and wondered what anyone could possibly be in a rush for at the top of this mountain.

Hubert explained that every team of astronomers in the world had booked some time on the telescope to carry out their observations. Another team was waiting to come and have their turn on the mountain. It was a little like the patients who made an appointment with Hector. You couldn't run late, otherwise everyone would be behind and the stars wouldn't be in the right place to be looked at any more.

'Then you have to rush to submit your paper before the next world conference. You spend nights in front of your computer . . .'

Hector understood a little better why Hubert's wife had upped and left one day.

He also thought that, truly, the Inuit and some of the world's other peoples didn't know how lucky they were never to be in a rush.

HECTOR AND THE JOURNEY INTO THE FUTURE

'SO,' said Hector, 'does looking at the stars teach us anything about time?'

'It should perhaps teach us inner peace,' said Hubert, 'but, as you know, it doesn't really.'

They went for a walk along a little path not far from the huge telescope, under a magnificent starry sky which could put you in mind of God. Hector remembered that the philosopher he liked, Pascal, when faced with these same infinitely far-off stars, had said: 'The silence of these eternal spaces terrifies me.' And yet Pascal believed in God.

Hubert explained different things to Hector. For a start, everything in the universe was so far away that even at the speed of light it would take for ever and a day to go from one place to another.

'For example,' said Hubert, 'if the sun went out all at once, we wouldn't even notice until eight minutes later. That's the time it takes the sun's light to reach us. And yet it's the closest star to us!'

'And what about the others, the ones that are further away?'

'Some died out millions of years ago,' said Hubert.

'But by the time the light reaches us, we see them as they were back then.'

My, my, thought Hector, so we've found a way to turn back time.

'So if you travelled a very long way from earth faster than the speed of light, you'd see earth as it was hundreds or thousands of years ago?'

'Yes, but it's impossible. Because you can't go faster than light. At best, if you could zoom off at the same speed as light, you'd still see the earth exactly as it was when you left it, so you wouldn't have got much out of going.'

'Why can't we go faster than light?'

'There are several answers to that. We are made of fairly heavy atoms. So we can't go faster than light, which itself has neither mass nor weight. You could also say that the faster a body goes, the more energy is needed to make it go faster, according to the general theory of relativity. So, when you approach the speed of light, you'd need infinite energy to go faster, and nothing and no one has infinite energy.'

Hector thought that Roger would have said that God has infinite energy, and that only God could have taken you back in time. Besides, He Himself had created it, according to different philosophers who believed in Him.

'So we can't go back in time?'

'Nope.'

'Can we travel into the future?'

'Oh yes,' said Hubert.

Amazing! thought Hector. People could travel into the future, but no one had mentioned it in the newspapers.

'But how?'

'Perhaps you know that the biggest discovery of relativity is that time doesn't go by everywhere always at the same speed.'

Hector vaguely remembered this.

'Basically, time goes by slower for you if you're going faster or if you're passing close by a very heavy body, like Earth for instance.'

'Do you have an example?'

'Yes, of course. If you were on a spacecraft travelling at close to the speed of light while I stayed on Earth, and I was able to look at your watch through a telescope, I'd see yours running more slowly than mine, even if we were wearing exactly the same type of watch . . .'

'And what about when I got back to Earth?'

'I'd be twenty years older than you, whereas from your point of view you'd only have been travelling for a few days.'

Hector thought to himself that this was the kind of time travel you didn't necessarily want to do! Travelling into the future and coming back to find all the people you loved very old, or even long since dead!

'And there'd be no going back,' added Hubert.

HECTOR AND THE LOTTERY TICKET

HECTOR asked Hubert if looking at the stars made you believe in God.

'Do you know the story about the first cosmonaut who came back to earth saying, "I journeyed into the heavens, but I never saw God or the angels"?'

'Yes.'

'Well, a surgeon, one who believed in God, replied, "I've operated on brains, but I've never seen a single *thought*!"'

Hector said to himself that, contrary to what psychiatrists sometimes said, some surgeons were really very intelligent.

They decided to head back, because it was beginning to get really cold, and Hector wished he was wearing the extra-warm anorak he'd had when he was with the Inuit.

'Some of my colleagues who believe in God say the proof that He exists is that *we* wouldn't exist if the laws of physics had been the slightest bit different.'

Hubert explained that the world worked according to three or four laws. Each one corresponded to a specific number that was called a constant, because it never changed. Hector remembered having learnt the 'g' constant for the law which explained how fast things fell, as the cable car might on the way back down. Hubert knew some other constants for more complicated laws, like the speed of light or how atoms fell together.

'Now, if these four constants were slightly different, the laws of physics wouldn't be the same. The universe couldn't have got started, if you like. The stars would have collapsed in on themselves and everything would have fused together. That's not the Big Bang any more, but the Big Crunch. Or else, everything would have vaporised. And so the Big Bang wouldn't have worked, and we wouldn't have a nice expanding universe with conditions for life on at least one planet, as we do now. They say it's not chance that the constants of physics are like that, out of millions of different possibilities, and it proves that God exists.'

'And what do you think of that?'

'If the laws were different, we wouldn't be here to wonder about the existence of God anyway. So, just because we're the result of one combination out of millions of possible combinations, it doesn't prove that it was God's choice. Similarly, if you buy the one ticket out of millions that wins the lottery, that doesn't prove that it was God's doing . . .'

'And you?' asked Hector.

'I believe in God,' said Hubert. 'But it doesn't have anything to do with all that,' he said, motioning towards the sky.

Just then, a young astronomer came to tell Hubert that he had to come and see something.

Hector followed them, but he was a little disappointed – he had been expecting to look at the stars through the telescope but these were just computer screens with all sorts of waves and numbers which scrolled by at top speed.

'We're verifying a hypothesis,' said Hubert.

He tried to explain the hypothesis to Hector: the more the stars moved away from each other, the faster and faster they did so . . . A little like: the more a person grows away from you, the faster and faster they do so, but Hector thought it best not to share this comparison with Hubert.

'And parallel universes?' asked Hector.

He was remembering Madame Irina and the shaman.

'That's a good question,' said Hubert.

'And are there any good answers?'

'Some physicists have thought that there isn't just one space-time, like the one in which I'm talking to you, here, now, but that there are others, each with a different probability of existence.'

'So it's possible?'

'Let's just say that it would be compatible with some theories put forward by some very serious people.'

Hector thought of Madame Irina and her little trains, and also the shaman and his journeys. Were they and others like them able to travel in the curvatures of space-times?

'Sometimes,' said Hubert, 'I tell myself that in a parallel universe my wife hasn't left me and we're very happy. But, just my luck, I'm stuck in the space-time where things turned out badly!'

Hector thought that if one day time travel became a possibility, psychiatrists would have a lot less work.

Before going to bed, he wrote:

Time Exercise No. 20: Read a good science book about time and the theory of relativity. Spend a bit of time understanding why if we can't go faster than the speed of light then we can't go back in time.

He remembered that a great scientist had written several books about this, and some of them had lovely pictures to help explain things. This scientist's body had been paralysed little by little by a terrible illness that doctors didn't yet know how to cure, but even though his body could no longer move much, that didn't stop his mind travelling alongside the light from the stars, the expanding universe and time.

HECTOR AND YING LI AT THE TOP OF THE MOUNTAIN

HECTOR was standing at the top of the mountain. He saw Ying Li coming to meet him on a little path. It was very cold and Ying Li was wrapped in a great big fur coat with a hood which made her look a bit like an Inuit.

She smiled as she got closer to Hector. Just then, he realised that they didn't need to actually speak, since they were speaking to each other in their thoughts. And Ying Li told him that, the other day, she'd wanted to thank him for changing her life, but she hadn't had the nerve.

Hector replied that it was life that had changed them both. Anyway, sooner or later, someone would have wanted to change Ying Li's life, because they would have wanted to save her from the situation she was in when Hector first met her. Ying Li gave a little nod, and in front of them appeared the softly lit bar where they'd met. But Hector couldn't see himself there, just lots of beautiful girls with men who were pleased with themselves, and Ying Li leaning her elbows on the bar right beside a Chinese man with his hair plastered back and a gold watch, who was drinking cognac and laughing as he stroked her arm. Ying Li was pretending to be happy and to find him funny. Then Hector saw her sitting on a bed in a hotel room looking sad, with a fat white man stark naked in the bathroom telling her with a laugh to come and join him. And then he saw her very late at night and very tired eating Chinese noodles in a little café with a friend who had too much make-up on and looked very tired too. He could see Ying Li at the bar again, with other men who were putting their arms round her waist and whispering in her ear, and then he saw her sitting on a big sofa in the shadows beside men who took her hand and fondled her breasts. And during this time Ying Li drank more and more cognac, and he saw her getting fatter and older. Then he saw her on a train arriving at quite a sad Chinese city with lots of factory chimney stacks, and he saw a big factory where Ying Li screwed little screws into little thingamajigs surrounded by hundreds of workers, and then, in the evening, he saw her coming home to quite a nice house where her mother and her two sisters lived, with a little shop that her mother ran, because that was what she had to show for all those years spent in bars and hotels – a nice house and a little shop – while the other workers went back to sleep in dormitories. And, in the evening, Ying Li helped her mother a bit in the little shop, and she also helped look after her sisters' children. Her sisters had husbands who also worked in the factory. But Ying Li didn't have a husband, because no husband would have wanted a girl who wasn't a spring chicken any more, and who'd spent too much time far away in the big city full of bars and hotels.

Hector realised that he'd just seen Ying Li's life without him, and that this life was as real as the other one, and that perhaps it existed in a parallel universe like those of Madame Irina and her friends, the presentists.

And, at the same time as he felt his heart go out to the Ying Li who was still living that life, he didn't know who to thank for having met the Ying Li who was standing beside him now. But *she* knew who to thank, because she gave Hector a little bow with her hands together as they did in the old monk's country before very respectable people, or before the statue they called the Enlightened One.

HECTOR CAN'T DREAM IN PEACE

JUST then, Hector woke up. The telephone was ringing in his bedroom. It was Édouard!

'It's the shaman again. Now he says you have to go to an island.'

'But I've just come from one,' said Hector, because the Chinese city he'd just come from was indeed an island.

'No, it can't be that one. The shaman said: "An island where the Kablunaks live a little like the Inuit."'

Hector couldn't hear Édouard very well, because there was lots of music and noise in the background. Édouard told him that he was in the last Kablunak town before Inuit country, where there were quite a few bars and some hotels.

'I'm not sure I'm completely cured,' said Édouard, who was having a bit of trouble with his words.

Hector remembered that, before, Édouard had been a regular at the softly lit bar where he'd met Ying Li.

He went back to sleep.

Hector was zooming along on a snowmobile with Roger, who seemed even more enormous muffled up in bearskins, and Noumen, the big dog, was bounding along beside them.

'What you have to understand,' said Roger, frowning,

'is that eternity isn't time which lasts for ever! Eternity is outside time; it encompasses the past, the present and the future all at once. Only God is eternal!'

At these words, Noumen looked at them with his pale eyes and said, 'Of course, but then what did God do before the world was created? Was there time then?'

'God sees the past, the present and the future at the same time,' said Roger. 'For Him, time doesn't go by. God is outside time, He's in eternity!'

'That doesn't answer my question,' said Noumen with a cheerful little yap.

'The present is just a reflection of eternity in time!' Roger cried out.

'Fine words,' retorted Noumen, 'but wouldn't the answer to the mystery of life in time and space lie outside time and space? If that's true, then where *does* the answer lie?'

Roger wanted to answer, but just then they went too fast over a big bump, and Roger and Hector and the snowmobile were catapulted into the air while Noumen barked and the telephone rang.

It was Clara.

'I had an awful dream,' said Clara, sounding all upset.

'Everything's fine,' said Hector. 'What kind of dream?'

'You didn't come back,' said Clara. 'You became a kind of monk with a shaved head and orange tunic, right at the top of a mountain. Lots of pretty Chinese women came to bow and pray to you.'

'That doesn't sound too awful,' said Hector, smiling.

'Stop it! It was awful, awful,' said Clara, laughing and crying at the same time.

Hector asked her how she was doing, and Clara said she was doing better. She had been to see old François, and they'd talked about time passing.

'He's going to write to you. But not to talk about me, of course.'

Old François couldn't talk to Hector about Clara. It was what they call doctor–patient confidentiality, and psychiatrists almost always respect it.

Afterwards, Hector tried to go back to sleep, but he couldn't.

An island where the Kablunaks live a little like the Inuit?

This time, he was back at the station on the mountain with the little wooden train, and the old Chinese man with the cap was holding his ticket out to him.

'Don't you recognise me?' he asked Hector.

No, Hector didn't recognise him . . .

Then the phone rang again. It was Marie-Agnès.

'Ahh,' she said, 'I've had a devil of a time getting hold of you.'

'Why not use the internet?' asked Hector, who was a little annoyed at being woken up for the third time.

'Oh, I've never really known how to work those things. Anyway, my Paul wanted to invite you to a big conference. A conference about time with lots of big names from different fields.'

Hector knew that these days, no matter what the

conference was about, somebody always invited a psychiatrist. It was a little like smoked salmon at a buffet: it isn't always good, but if there isn't any, people will miss it. So he didn't much fancy going to this conference.

'Look,' said Marie-Agnès, 'I can tell that you're not wildly enthusiastic about it, but I'd really like you to come.'

'Why?'

'My Paul's just had a massive panic attack. I found him shaking all over when I woke up, and really not happy at all. "I control everything," he told me, "and yet I control nothing." I knew right away that he was in a bad way. So I thought it would do him good to see you, and pretty quickly too. But, of course, he'll never admit that he needs to see a psychiatrist . . . So I told him I was going to call you, about the conference . . .'

Marie-Agnès told him where she and Paul were waiting for him to come and join them, and then Hector knew for sure that he had to go there straight away.

An island where the Kablunaks live a little like the Inuit!

HECTOR MEETS AN IMPORTANT MAN

'I'M very glad you came,' said Paul. 'I'm sorry we only let you know at the last minute.'

Behind Paul, Hector could see the columns of a ruined temple outlined against the deep blue of the sea. Marie-Agnès, Paul and he were sitting on a stone bench which, in the shade of an olive tree, looked almost as old as the temple.

Marie-Agnès seemed delighted – she was very proud to show off her wonderful Paul to Hector and to show off her brilliant psychiatrist to Paul, and also to think that perhaps they were going to get on well.

Still, Hector had noticed the flicker of panic in Paul's eyes. He wondered when they'd have the chance to talk about it.

'Your name isn't on the programme yet, but we're printing a new one right now. We'll have it in . . . a few minutes,' said Paul, looking at his watch.

At first sight, Paul hardly looked much older than Hector. Hector could see that he didn't have any grey hair at all, but now, thanks to the nurse's remark, he knew that this just meant Paul had an excellent hairdresser. Hector could also see that Paul had practically none of those little wrinkles around his eyes. He wondered if it was because he'd found an anti-ageing cream that was better than all the rest, or if his doctor or surgeon colleagues had managed to smooth away those signs of ageing.

Paul talked quickly and fidgeted a lot in his chair. Under his shirt, you could make out real muscles, and you got the feeling he kept in shape by working out. So, all in all, you might have thought he was much younger than he really was. Except in certain lights, Hector had noticed. When the light hit him from above, like in this blazing sunshine, you could suddenly see that Paul's face was that of a man his age (that's to say, a good dog and a half more than Hector).

Time Exercise No. 21, thought Hector: *If you want to look young, always stay in the shade (or in candlelight).*

But, as Hector knew that Paul didn't like feeling as if he was wasting time, Hector thought he would write this exercise down later.

'So,' said Marie-Agnès, 'what do you think?'

Hector looked at the programme of the conference Paul had organised. It was called 'Time on Our Side'. There were different speakers, all quite famous. They were going to talk about time, from their point of view of course. There was a philosopher with tousled hair, a monk from Hector's religion, a big consultant for big companies who was an expert in time, a top biologist who was going to explain why we get old, and a racing driver who won

144

by taking corners a few tenths of a second faster than his rivals.

Then Paul was going to speak himself, since he was the one organising this big conference which lots of people from his big company had been invited to. And quite a few journalists too, or rather journalists' bosses, because Paul really hoped people would talk about this conference and, as a result, about his big company.

What did Paul's big company make? All kinds of beauty creams, including the most famous anti-ageing cream, and also hair dye, and lots of products to make men and women all over the world look younger and more beautiful. Hundreds of researchers worked day in, day out mixing lots of ingredients in different-coloured test tubes in order to come up with better and better products.

All the guests were staying in an old village very close to the temple. At one time, it had been an ordinary village with local people living there, but gradually it had become impossible to make a living from fishing, and the village had been deserted. Later, the locals who still lived on the island had done up the village to attract people from elsewhere, just like this conference. Before, they'd fished for seafood, now, they fished for tourists.

'I think the programme looks very good,' said Hector. 'Different points of view . . . people won't feel as if they're wasting their time.'

'They won't, will they?' said Paul with a relieved smile.

A young woman dressed like Clara when she was going

to work appeared, holding a bundle of new programmes over her head to shield her from the sun, and struggling over the stony path in her high heels. Paul checked that Hector's name was indeed on the programme, and then the two of them started talking about the seating arrangements for dinner.

'So, how about going for a walk?' said Marie-Agnès, who was obviously thoroughly bored by these organisational issues.

From the top of the hill where they were standing, there was a good view of the little fishing harbour which, for a long time, had provided a living for everyone on the island. There were still quite a few boats painted in cheerful colours, and Hector saw some fishermen unloading their fish, which shimmered in the sun. A little further away, old people were sitting on benches in the shade of the trees, watching children playing with a ball against the wall of the church.

An island where the Kablunaks live like the Inuit, the shaman had said.

Hector thought to himself that Clara would have liked it here.

All the same, he wondered why the shaman had wanted him to come to this island, because, unlike the salmon which was one day going to end up on the buffet, Hector's Being-in-the-world was both open to the future and beset by Concern, as the famous philosopher with the little moustache would have put it.

HECTOR IS WORKING, EVEN
BY THE SEA

In the end, Marie-Agnès left Hector alone with Paul. They went to have a drink in the villa where Marie-Agnès and Paul were staying. The closed shutters let in a bit of sun and it cast a lovely light that would have made anyone look young.

Hector felt like having a beer, but, as Paul had poured himself a glass of vegetable juice, he did the same. He also saw that Paul looked relieved to be alone with him.

'Always put on a brave face . . .' said Paul, sighing.

With just a few questions, Hector put him at ease – after all, it was his job.

And Paul told him quite quickly that he wasn't feeling at all good. For nearly a week, he'd been having massive panic attacks every morning.

'I normally get up very early and have my coffee while I think over my plans for the day. But there, facing the sea, I felt terrible, as if I was going to die. There I was, shaking, heart pounding in my chest, bathed in sweat and everything. But that's nothing. I have the feeling that my life is getting away from me. That everything's pointless. That time is ticking away, and there's nothing I can do about it, and that I'm going . . . straight into the void.'

Hector could see that just by talking about his panic attack Paul was working himself up into another one. Hector suggested that he lie down on the sofa for a minute and take deep breaths.

Paul managed to calm himself down a little, and then he started talking again, looking up at the ceiling.

'All my life, I've fought against time!' said Paul. 'I was quick at school. And later on I always measured myself against my colleagues of the same age. Which of us was going to be a general manager first? That's the sort of question we'd ask ourselves. I was very proud of being a CEO at thirty-two. Then I ran bigger and bigger companies. Of course, I've been divorced twice. But, hey, my children are doing fine. The company went global . . . and everyone says it's down to me. But the other morning . . .'

'The other morning?' asked Hector. (We'll let you in on a psychiatrist trick: when people stop talking, repeat just the end of their last sentence.)

'. . . I felt that all that was completely empty. Yes, I did that; I got there. But now I'm an old bloke who tries to believe, and make others believe, that he's still young. What is the point of everything I've achieved, if right now I feel so awful? After all, if I hadn't achieved all that, somebody else would more than likely have done just as well. In any case, the beauty market is booming, so whether it was me or somebody else it would have worked . . .'

Hector knew that when people like Paul became modest, they weren't far from very deep depression.

'. . . The other morning, I felt as if my whole life had just been empty all along. And yet I thought it was very full. I've always wanted to fill time. Fill time! But I don't believe in that any more . . . Even when you fill it, it still slips through your fingers. And off we go, off we go, straight into the void!' said Paul, sitting bolt upright on the sofa, a little like someone who wants to jump from the car before it goes over the edge of the ravine.

Hector said to himself that Paul needed to talk quite a lot, in several sittings, but before that he needed to get a bit better. So he gave him some little pills that he always carried around with him just in case. Some had pretty much the same thing in them as the ones he'd given to Fernand's dog. (But Hector didn't tell Paul that, of course.)

Later, he wrote in his little notebook:

Time Exercise No. 22: In your opinion, what is a very full life?

HECTOR GOES BACK TO SCHOOL

And so the conference began.

Paul had expected Hector to speak in the morning, but Hector explained to him that psychiatrists were rarely at their best in the morning (otherwise, they would have become surgeons). So he was only going to speak at the end of the third day, just before dinner.

Everyone – a good hundred people, Hector reckoned – was sitting on the stone seats of an amphitheatre as old as the temple. Luckily, the seats had been covered with lovely blue cushions that were very comfortable. Above them, a big blue and white awning shielded them from the sun, and local women in blue dresses and white aprons often brought refreshments.

In a way, it was lucky that old François wasn't there, thought Hector, because in the different countries around the world where they'd been to conferences Hector had noticed that his old colleague always had a soft spot for the pretty local waitresses who weren't aware how beautiful they were. And here he noticed a few of those, and also some pretty journalists or journalists' bosses.

We're not going to tell you every little thing about the conference, because that would be a bit boring. Hector was rather bored himself, a bit like when he was at school trying to listen to his teachers. And yet he knew it was interesting, but that's the way it was — he liked listening to people telling him their life stories, but when it came to lectures he'd rather read them, not listen to them.

'You don't seem all that interested in this,' said Marie-Agnès, who was sitting beside him.

'Of course I am,' said Hector.

To help himself concentrate, he decided to write down the most interesting things in his little notebook. Here are his notes.

The philosopher

Very complicated. But some interesting questions. Is time like space? Both were created by God at the same time as the world. Leibniz, for example, thought this, but Newton considered time to be an attribute of God, that, like Him, had always existed. They argued about this, and Newton was quite mean. Or are time and space just ideas invented by man to make sense of the world in his own way? For Kant or Spinoza, time only exists through us. So time wouldn't exist without us to feel it or measure it? If you ask me, it did exist before us, because otherwise how would we have had time to come into being? On this point, I think I'd agree more with Aristotle and Hobbes, less with St Augustine and Kant, but I've already sort of forgotten what they said.

Lots of philosophers from the last century thought very hard about this problem: it takes time to be, and if time didn't exist we wouldn't have the time to be. And as

soon as we come into being then there's time. And so, for
some people, being and time were one and the same, and
they'd write whole books to explain why. Heidegger (little
moustache), Sartre (big round glasses). Philosophy is
all well and good, but it's a little like maths: you need to
work at it every day to appreciate it. And take up German.
Shame no one talked about the theory of relativity —
they should have invited an expert in stars like Hubert.
Mention this to Paul for next time.

Beside him, he saw Marie-Agnès was having a little
snooze, and it reminded him that philosophers were
mostly men. Or else the women who were philosophers
often questioned not what was true or false, but what was
good or bad for people. And therefore for babies, when it
came down to it.

The time expert for big companies
Too simple. His big thing: telling the difference between
what's urgent and what's important. Important and
urgent: do it straight away. Important and not urgent:
think about it a little every day. Urgent and not important:
give it to someone else. Not important and not urgent: toss
it overboard as quickly as possible. Very happy to say
that, with today's means of communication, everything
goes everywhere faster, but he's forgetting that we could
have said the same thing before, when people learnt to ride
horses or when the telephone was invented. Likes saying
words like 'instantaneity', 'hypertime' and 'world-time'.

A woman asked the time expert a question, wondering if all these devices which allowed people to speak to each other, write to each other and even see each other at any time anywhere in the world weren't going to put an end to time for thinking things over.

'Not at all,' said the time expert with a big smile. 'Quite the opposite . . . by working faster, we free up time for ourselves!'

Hector wasn't so sure. He remembered Clara constantly checking her mobile phone or her internet messages, even at weekends.

Marie-Agnès also asked a question.

'This urgent-important thing of yours is interesting,' she said. 'But when you say urgent or important, urgent or important for who? Me? My boss? God?'

'I don't know about God,' said the time expert, laughing. 'It's up to you to define your own priorities.'

Hector told himself that he wasn't going to leave Marie-Agnès to ask all the questions by herself. He wanted to give her the impression that she'd been right to get Paul to invite him.

By seeing patients who talked to him about their jobs and also friends who worked a little like Clara, he'd ended up with a pretty good idea of how people decided what was urgent and what was important, and also of the men and women it worked for best.

He raised his finger and was handed the microphone. He explained that at work, for example, it was important to tell the difference between three kinds of important things: firstly, things that are important for doing your job well; secondly, things that are important for your boss; and, thirdly, those that are important for your career.

'In an ideal world,' said Hector, 'they should be exactly the same!'

This made everyone laugh: people knew all too well that they didn't live in an ideal world! Hector had often noticed that people who put 'job done well' first were generally rewarded less than those who put 'important for my boss' first, or 'important for my career'. Then these conscientious people often got really down because they hadn't been rewarded, and yet they felt they had done their job well. Hector helped them think about other priorities: what was important for their boss or their career. As to their boss, they also had to work out what was the most important thing for him: doing his job well, his own boss or his career. Then you could also try to work out how your boss's boss thought, but that got a bit complicated, like the theory of relativity.

'But,' somebody said, 'I don't really understand the difference between important for my career and important for my boss, since it's my boss who decides my career.'

'Not just your boss,' said Hector.

For your career, you had to spend a little time getting to know other bosses besides your own, keep up with what was happening elsewhere, make friends and learn new things that would be useful later on.

'Like learning Chinese,' somebody piped up.

Hector was pleased, because people looked as if they'd found his little remarks interesting.

While they were waiting for the biologist who was going to explain why we get old, Hector took out his little notebook.

Time Exercise No. 23: Draw up a nice table with four boxes: Urgent-Important, Urgent-Not important, Not Urgent-Important, Not urgent-Not important. Put everything you have to do into these boxes. Are you any further forward?

Afterwards, he felt quite pleased to add his own little exercise:

Time Exercise No. 24: Sort out everything you have to do into 'important for doing your job well', 'important for your boss' and 'important for your career'. How much time do you spend on each of the three?

Suddenly, it occurred to Hector that you could also apply this to family life.

Time Exercise No. 24(B): Work out how much time you spend doing important things for your children, for your partner and for yourself. Show the rest of your family the results.

He was aware that this was rather a dangerous exercise to do for harmony at home, and thought that he wouldn't recommend it to everyone.

After that, he began to get a bit bored again, but luckily the biologist had come up on stage. He was a tall, serious-looking chap, and Hector thought he was bound to have some interesting things to say to explain why we get old, and how we can't help it.

HECTOR LEARNS WHY WE GET OLD

The biologist
Very interesting on all the reasons we get old. The most important: our cells constantly reproduce by dividing in two. But each time it's a little like a photocopy of a photocopy: the copy isn't quite as good. So each new generation of cells doesn't work quite as well as the last. This means that little by little our body doesn't work quite as well and we get old. And this never-ending photocopying of cells is controlled by the ends of our chromosomes, the telomeres. So if we could control how telomeres behave, the photocopies would be perfect, the new cell would be identical to the last, and we'd never get old ever again; we'd stop at the age we're at . . .

'That's brilliant!' said Marie-Agnès.

'We're working on it,' whispered Paul, who had come back to sit beside her.

Hector felt a bit dizzy thinking about what would happen if we could control telomeres. People would swallow a pill and, hey presto, they'd stay the age they were at for ever. But for those who were very old already it wouldn't be so funny. And for young people – what age should they decide to stop at? And, besides, who'd have access to these pills? Rich people first, most likely, who would live much longer than the poor, once again. Would this trigger wars? Being killed or dying in an accident would be a much greater tragedy than before, because your life would really be cut short by hundreds of years. Then would people perhaps become very, very fearful and never dare do anything a bit risky ever again? Wouldn't we end up getting bored with living? And in a society where everyone was young, wouldn't youth eventually lose its ephemeral and wonderful charm? And if no one died of old age any more, how would we feed all the babies that came into the world? Stop having babies? And if no one had children, what would that do to people? Wouldn't they become very selfish, and so not as happy?

We'll know when we get there, thought Hector, but he wasn't sure he wanted to get there. On the other hand, never seeing himself growing old with Clara . . .

Just then, the biologist put up a slide.

It was a big fat white worm, not very appetising, it has to be said, and Hector thought it wasn't a very good idea to show it just before dinner.

'Normally, this type of worm lives for three months,' said the biologist. Hector felt a little shiver run down his spine, sensing what was coming next.

'But we've been working on the telomeres of its chromosomes, which are much simpler than ours.'

The biologist paused for a moment and then he said, 'That worm has been alive for a year.'

Everyone went 'Oooh'. Hector wondered what the

old monk would have made of all this, and, besides, where was he anyway, and why had the shaman wanted him to come to this island?

'Right, let's go and have dinner,' said Marie-Agnès. 'You'll see, the menu's great.'

And Hector was sure that there would only be good fats on the menu. It made him happy to think of all those cows, all those sheep and all those pigs that could keep enjoying their Being-in-the-world, carefree.

HECTOR REALISES THAT
DIET ISN'T EVERYTHING IN LIFE

THAT night, Hector didn't have any dreams.

But he woke up very early in the morning and decided to go for a walk round the village and see the fishing boats before the sun started beating down too fiercely.

On the way, he bumped into the biologist, who must have had the same idea.

'I'm curious to know what you're going to be talking about tomorrow at the conference,' said the biologist.

'Me too,' said Hector.

And the biologist laughed, thinking this was a good joke. But it was true: Hector still didn't really know what he was going to say, but he told himself that he had almost two days to think about it, so why rush? When it came down to it, it was important-but-not-yet-urgent; he just had to think about it from time to time. Important for whom, anyway? The biologist, who was called Olivier, was a tall thin man with hollow cheeks, and he also seemed quite young, even though Hector guessed that he was at least one dog older than him. Hector wondered if, in the evenings, at home, Olivier did experiments on his telomeres to stay young.

'Do you know why this island is special?' asked Olivier, as they reached the village square.

A little market had been set up, with people who had come over from the mainland to sell things you couldn't make on the island – lamps, sewing machines, coffee, even print dresses, Hector noticed.

'No, I don't,' said Hector.

'It's one of the places in the world with the highest number of people older than a hundred.'

Hector looked around him. In the shade of the plane trees, you could see some very old men and very old ladies sitting on their benches – among them, most likely some centenarians – while, at the quayside, fishermen were talking near their nets and their crates full of fish. A little further off, some women were going to the market. And everywhere children had begun playing and chasing after each other because it was Sunday and there was no school.

The church clock very softly chimed seven o'clock.

Hector and Olivier decided to go and have a coffee at a little pavement café, which also served as a grocer's-cum-tobacconist's-tackle shop-bike rental shop.

The lady who ran the café (who, surprisingly, looked a little like Ying Li's mother in Hector's dream) asked them if they'd like something to eat, and they said yes.

As well as coffee, they got some slices of very tasty quite dark bread, a little dish of olive oil, two or three fresh tomatoes and a little jar of pickled herrings.

'And there's the secret!' exclaimed Olivier. 'Their diet! Vegetables, fish, nuts. Only good fats!'

Hector remembered that this type of diet was called a

Mediterranean diet. Not surprising really, since this island was in the middle of the sea called the Mediterranean!

'And another thing: they don't eat much – less than we do. If you underfeed rats a little, they live longer.'

Looking at Olivier's hollow cheeks, Hector thought that he, too, must have been trying not to eat too much.

'If everyone from our country began to eat less, it would add at least ten years to our lives,' said Olivier, swallowing a pickled herring.

That's as may be, thought Hector, but to live in hunger?

Hector kept looking around him at the children playing, the men unloading a crate of fish every now and then when the conversation died down, the women talking amongst themselves about the right sewing machine to buy, and the old men and old ladies sitting not far away on their benches. Some of them were probably watching their great-great-grandchildren.

Hector also remembered that a long time ago on this and all the other neighbouring islands, before the arrival of Hector's religion, people used to think that life began again after death, and that the whole world even began again from time to time, like the sun, which came up every morning.

An island where the Kablunaks live like the Inuit.

Hector understood that the Mediterranean diet was certainly very good for you, but that there were other explanations for the number of centenarians on this island. This was going to give him some good ideas for what he was going to say at the conference.

HECTOR HAS A REST

WHEN he got back to his room, since he still didn't know why he was there, Hector decided to make some phone calls. (Actually, he did know why: because Paul and Marie-Agnès had asked him to come, but rather like a conversation which is really secretly about something else, he thought there was another reason hidden behind this reason, and the shaman must have known what it was. It reminded him of the question asked by a philosopher, whom the philosopher at the conference had talked about, in fact: why is there a universe rather than nothing at all?)

First of all, he called Clara.

She told him she was feeling better and that she missed him. Hector was so happy he felt tears well up in his eyes, but he pulled himself together, because men don't cry, except at their friends' funerals. He told Clara that he missed her lots too, and that he was hoping to come home very soon. They sent kisses over the phone and, once again, Hector felt huge waves of love flowing between them at the speed of light, as if time had never existed, and they were back at the beginning of their relationship.

Then he tried to call Édouard, which wasn't very easy, as you can imagine. In the end, Édouard called back a few minutes later.

'I'm back at the camp,' he said.

Hector pictured him in the big tent where he'd had breakfast with Hilton and Éléonore, near the devices that let people talk to each other anywhere in the world, and which the time expert loved so much.

'What about the shaman?' asked Hector.

'He gave us a real fright,' said Édouard.

He explained that the shaman had not only drunk too much lichen beer, but also some vodka that the Inuit had got from another Inuit village. Now he was lying motionless on a bed in the Kablunak camp infirmary with quite a lot of machines blinking all around him to make sure that he didn't go to sleep for good.

'The doctor says he'll pull through.'

This turn of events proved that shamans – a little like psychiatrists, for that matter – could be very clever when it came to others, but not so clever when it came to themselves.

So there was no new message from the shaman and Hector wasn't much further forward.

Then he called old François.

'I've hitched my wagon again to a little train that I love so much. And, for the time being, I'm not thinking about the end of the line at all any more! Heidegger would give me a bad mark!'

Hector wondered what the new little locomotive looked like that could make such an old carriage so happy.

Without wanting to say much because of doctor–patient confidentiality, old François told Hector that Clara was doing better.

She wouldn't be needing any little pills, but it would be a good idea for Hector to come back fairly soon to see her.

'As you know, dear friend, in love timing is everything!'

Hector thought this was very well said and vowed to make a note of it in his notebook.

Anyway, to cut a long story short, everything was fine, and, as Hector had got up quite early for a psychiatrist, he thought he'd lie down for five minutes on his bed and have a little rest before going to the conference to listen to the first speaker: a monk from his religion, then later on the racing driver.

But he fell asleep, which was a bit of a shame, because those people were bound to have had some interesting things to say.

HECTOR AND THE TWO
CENTENARIANS

HECTOR was lying on a bed, a little tube up his nose, another bigger one down his throat, and little wires stuck all over his body to monitor his heartbeat and his breathing. Machines were blinking all around him.

The hardest thing was that he couldn't move at all, or speak. And yet he felt wide awake, and he could even hear the wind of the ice field outside. He saw a young woman coming towards him; it was an Inuit nurse with a little white cap, and without warning she shone a little torch right into his eye, then into his other eye, and it was very unpleasant, but he couldn't say anything to her. She disappeared from view, but since he couldn't move his head she might still have been very close by for all he knew.

It was really very hard to lie awake without being able to move, with just the beep-beep of the machines all around him.

The only way to escape would have been by dreaming, but how do you dream without sleeping?

Hector concentrated hard, and then it worked, and he was back at the village square, right by the church, and he could see Olivier walking away, swallowing pickled herrings, which he tossed up into the air ahead of him as he went, which made the children who were running around him laugh a lot.

On a bench in the shade of a plane tree, he saw two old men from the village watching him. He decided to go and talk to them.

They were smiling as they watched him coming towards them. They looked very old, so old that even their wrinkles had faded away a little. Their eyes were cloudy, but they seemed pleased to see Hector all the same. He said to himself they had to be centenarians.

'You've come a fair distance, eh?' said the centenarian who was wearing a cap.

'I like travelling.'

'Us too,' said the one with the beret, the same kind of beret people used to wear a long time ago in Hector's country.

Hector and the two centenarians spoke the same language, even though it was difficult to tell which one.

'Come out of the sun and sit down or you'll get heatstroke,' said the centenarian with the cap.

Hector was happy to sit in the shade, because the fox furs were beginning to make him hot.

And they kept watching the children who were playing in the square and the boats which kept coming in on the deep-blue sea.

'I wonder if they'll live as long as us,' said the centenarian with the cap.

'They'll have better medicine,' said the one wearing the beret.

'But they won't have the same life either . . . they'll always be in a rush.'

'And maybe they won't eat properly. And they might also end up more alone.'

'And then, one day, they'll go into an old people's home.'

Then they didn't say anything at all for a moment. You got the feeling that the idea of an old people's home made them quite sad.

'Maybe they'll get used to it in the end,' said the centenarian with the cap.

'Maybe, but only seeing old people all day . . .'

'That's a bit of an exaggeration – there's the staff too.'

'Yes, but can you imagine being stuck in a room, instead of having all this?' said the centenarian with the beret, sweeping his hand across the blue sky, the square, the boats, the sea and the children.

And he took off his beret, uncovering a very handsome shock of white hair. Hector also noticed that he was wearing a bow tie.

'I have a question for you,' said Hector.

'A question?' said the centenarian with the bow tie. 'It's been a long time since I've been asked one of those.'

'I enjoy questions . . . it's the answers that tire me out,' said the centenarian with the cap.

'All right then,' said Hector. 'In your opinion, what is a very full life?'

The two centenarians looked at each other and burst

out laughing. It was a pleasure to watch, but Hector wasn't much further forward.

Finally, the centenarian with the bow tie stopped laughing and said very seriously, 'This idea of a very full life is dangerous. Because you can't ever fill it as much as you'd like to. And you also fill it with mistakes, inevitably. What counts is sometimes feeling your life is full. Or, rather, living some moments to the full, if you like.'

'And, what's more, to live fully in the present, you have to empty your mind often,' said the centenarian with the cap.

Hector understood what he meant. He knew that to enjoy the moment you had to let yourself be fully immersed in it, and not worry about other things.

'Life isn't like a bottle you can fill,' said the centenarian with the bow tie, 'but more like a piece of music, with some less successful or boring moments, and others which are more intense. Music is a very good way of thinking about time. A note only moves you because you remember the one before, and you're waiting for the next . . . Each one only means something wrapped in a bit of the past and the future.'

The centenarian with the bow tie started to whistle, and straight away the centenarian with the cap joined in.

Hector recognised a tune composed by a great musician who wore a wig and who must have felt that he'd had a very full life: he'd invented hundreds of pieces of music and, at the same time, he'd been father to twenty children!

He didn't have his notebook with him, but he resolved to write:

> *Time Exercise No. 25: Listen to some music and tell yourself that it's the same thing as time. Compare it with your life.*

HECTOR AND HISTORY, WHICH
KEEPS REPEATING ITSELF

AT that point, the lady who ran the little café came out of it and walked towards them.

'Whistling is all very well, but perhaps it's time to think about lunch,' she told them.

'Oh, we've got plenty of time,' said the centenarian with the bow tie.

'You should rustle some up for our friend too,' said the centenarian with the cap, pointing at Hector.

'I have,' said the woman.

And she walked away.

'Trust her to try and rush us!' said the centenarian with the bow tie.

'She means well . . . she's just a little like her mother. And like her grandmother too, as I remember.'

'How can you remember, since you're not from around here?' said the centenarian with the bow tie.

'You aren't either,' said the centenarian with the cap.

'Oh yes, that's true . . .'

And they both looked at Hector.

'Are you going to be leaving again soon?' asked the centenarian with the bow tie.

'I don't know,' said Hector. 'I'm happy to be here, but I don't know why I came.'

'I don't think you'll be staying for long,' said the centenarian with the cap, giving a little sigh.

Just then, Hector realised that his cap was a station master's cap, which was strange because there weren't any trains on the island.

'Are you a station master?' asked Hector.

'Temporarily,' said the centenarian with the station master's cap.

'He's still working,' said the centenarian with the bow tie.

'But not for much longer,' said the centenarian with the cap.

'And what if I wanted to take the train from your station?' asked Hector.

'Then you'd better be quick, because, you know, I won't be around for very much longer,' said the centenarian with the cap, giving a little laugh.

And, just then, Hector recognised him.

One of the machines around him in the room started making a noise and he expected to see the nurse coming. But, no, it was the telephone.

Hector answered it.

'What happened to you?' asked Marie-Agnès. 'You missed the monk.'

'Was it interesting?'

'Oh yes, I learnt the difference between eternity, sempiternity and aeviternity.'

'You can tell me about it,' said Hector. 'I'm on my way.'

But first he called Trevor and Katharine. It was Trevor who answered.

'Have you been back on the little train that goes up to the monastery?' asked Hector.

'I haven't, but yesterday Katharine went up there again with some friends.'

'Is the old man who hands out the tickets still there?'

Trevor called Katharine over to the phone.

'No, he wasn't,' said Katharine. 'It was a young man. He told me that the old Chinese man was too tired.'

'I'm on my way,' said Hector.

He realised that Paul and Marie-Agnès wouldn't be over the moon, but they'd understand. And perhaps old François would have time to get here by tomorrow with his new little locomotive, who would no doubt be delighted to find herself on such a beautiful island, and look on admiringly as old François said intelligent things. He was sure that old François would go and talk to a centenarian on a village bench.

And, if that wasn't possible, it would no doubt give the time expert the chance to say 'instantaneity' and put old François up on a big TV screen in the middle of the amphitheatre. Before that, the girl who struggled over the stony path in her heels would come and see Paul again on his bench in the morning with a pile of freshly printed new programmes, which proved that perhaps history kept repeating itself without ever getting any better, and you needed to be very brave to cope with this eternal return, as the philosopher with the enormous moustache once said.

Hector remembered his name too: Nietzsche.

HECTOR IS A GOOD DOCTOR

THE next day, before he left, Hector went to see Paul. They both had coffee looking at the sea, which was a very pale blue, exactly the same colour as the sky at the North Pole when the sun was about to come up, thought Hector. Or the colour of Éléonore's eyes, but he quickly put that thought out of his mind.

'Your pills have calmed me down,' said Paul. 'But I'm still asking myself the same questions.'

'About how full your life is?'

'Yes. I've been thinking that it's fuller than I thought, but there are still quite a few things missing. And there's a hole at the bottom of the bottle!'

All the same, Paul was managing to laugh at himself a little, so he was a bit better.

'Instead of a bottle,' said Hector, 'try comparing your life to music.'

And he told Paul what the centenarians had revealed to him in his dream (without saying it was a dream, of course, because Hector was supposed to be a modern psychiatrist, not a shaman, or, in any case, that's not how Paul saw him).

'Time is like music?' asked Paul, with a look of amazement.

'Exactly,' said Hector. 'Each note only means something because of the note before and the note after. A note is like the present, which never stops becoming the past. And yet music exists!'

Later, as he walked away, he heard Paul starting to whistle.

Quite out of tune as it happens but, wouldn't you know, this music was also composed by the great musician with twenty children and a very full life!

HECTOR DRINKS TOO MUCH

ÉLÉONORE opened the little notebook and began to read.

Time Exercise No. 1: Measure your life in dogs.

Time Exercise No. 2: Make a list of what you wanted to do when you were little and dreaming of being grown up.

Time Exercise No. 3: Over the course of one day, count how much time you have for yourself. Sleeping doesn't count (unless it's at the office).

Time Exercise No. 4: Think of all the people and things you are not paying enough attention to now, because one day they will be gone and then it will be too late.

Time Exercise No. 5: Imagine your life as a big roll of fabric, from which you have made all the clothes you have worn since you were little. Imagine the set of clothes you could make with the rest of the roll.

Time Exercise No. 6: Write down everything that makes you feel younger. Then write down everything that makes you feel older.

Time Exercise No. 7: If you don't believe in the good Lord, imagine you do. If you do believe in Him, imagine you no longer believe. Note how this affects your view of time going by.

Time Exercise No. 8: Play a game with some friends. Try to find a definition of time. First prize: a watch.

Time Exercise No. 9: Take some time to think about things. The past has gone, so it doesn't exist. The future hasn't happened yet, so it doesn't exist. The present doesn't exist, because, as soon as you talk about it, it's already in the past. So, what does exist?

Time Exercise No. 10: What if your life was just someone else's dream? In that case, where are they sleeping?

Time Exercise No. 11: Hide your watch. From time to time, make a note of what time you think it is. Then compare it with the time on your watch.

Time Exercise No. 12: Thinking about your past, try to predict your future (at least, your most probable future).

Time Exercise No. 13: Whenever you meet an elderly person, always imagine what they were like when they were young.

Time Exercise No. 14: Imagine that growing old will bring you closer to the Kingdom of Heaven (or the place in your religion).

Time Exercise No. 15: Imagine you are a cow. You don't remember that you were little. You don't know that you're going to die. Would you be happy? If you could choose, would you rather be a cow? Or maybe another animal? Which kind?

Time Exercise No. 16: Concentrate and be aware that there's no time without movement, and no movement without time. Time is a measure of movement.

Time Exercise No. 17: Put together a collection of beautiful poems about time going by. Learn them by heart and recite them to friends who are older and younger than you.

Time Exercise No. 18: Do you spend time trying to change the things that can be changed? Do you try to accept the things that can't? Do you know the difference between them? Make sure you can answer 'yes' to these three questions.

Time Exercise No. 19: Meet the children of the women you ~~love~~ loved when you were younger.

Time Exercise No. 20: Read a good science book about

time and the theory of relativity. Spend a bit of time understanding why if we can't go faster than the speed of light then we can't go back in time.

Time Exercise No. 21: If you want to look young, always stay in the shade (or in candlelight).

Time Exercise No. 22: In your opinion, what is a very full life?

Time Exercise No. 23: Draw up a nice table with four boxes: Urgent-Important, Urgent-Not important, Not Urgent-Important, Not urgent-Not important. Put everything you have to do into these boxes. Are you any further forward?

Time Exercise No. 24: Sort out everything you have to do into 'important for doing your job well', 'important for your boss' and 'important for your career'. How much time do you spend on each of the three?

Time Exercise No. 24(B): Work out how much time you spend doing important things for your children, for your partner and for yourself. Show the rest of your family the results.

Time Exercise No. 25: Listen to some music and tell yourself that it's the same thing as time. Compare it with your life.

Éléonore read on a bit, then she shut the little notebook and said, 'I wouldn't want to seem like I'm criticising, but your take on philosophy is a little sketchy!'

'It's a summary. And, besides it's not finished.'

'So,' said Édouard, 'what's next – Pinot or Cabernet?'

'I'll let you choose,' said Hector.

And Édouard called the Chinese wine waiter over again.

The three of them were having dinner in a beautiful restaurant with windows on all sides at the top of a hotel. You could see the Chinese city glittering in the night, and even a little beacon at the top of the mountain so that planes wouldn't bump into it.

When he'd set off for China again, Hector had called Édouard. He thought that two heads would be better than one in the search for the old monk. And, also, he didn't want to be all by himself again in the Chinese city. Otherwise, he might have called Ying Li a second time.

'You two don't half knock it back!' said Éléonore.

The problem was that Éléonore had come along with Édouard, at first just because she'd flown him quite far south in her little plane, then because she'd said that she needed a holiday and so why not come along with Édouard? Édouard had said why not indeed?

'You know that alcohol makes you age?' said Éléonore.

Hector and Édouard looked at each other.

'Maybe we're not afraid of time passing,' said Hector.

'It's more that you're men and you know that you'll

always find a woman who'll love your wrinkles, or at least pretend not to see them!'

'Maybe drinking makes us forget about time going by,' said Édouard.

Around them, at other tables, there were quite a few very well-dressed Chinese men and women who were busy forgetting about time going by. Édouard had explained to Hector that it was China and Japan that had saved cognac, and, there, you could see that they were still going strong.

They had all arrived in China very late in the evening, too late to go and see who was handing out the tickets for the little train. Until the next morning, they didn't have much to do, other than have interesting conversations.

Éléonore had started to read the list of time exercises that Hector had written in his little notebook.

'You've reinvented or remembered, maybe' (Hector wasn't sure which it was either!) 'Aristotle and St Augustine: "There's a past present, a future present and a present present."'

Hector was impressed. Éléonore explained that apart from learning how to fly a plane she had also studied philosophy.

'I wanted to understand what the point of living was,' said Éléonore.

Once again, Hector thought that Éléonore must have had a few problems with her mother or father, or both.

'What St Augustine realised,' Éléonore continued, her eyes shining with excitement, 'is that everything only exists in the present. The past and the future only exist when they're in the present. Some people say that the present doesn't exist, but you could say the opposite . . . nothing exists outside the present! You can only live in the present; there's no getting away from the present. Whatever you think, whatever you do, it's always today!'

Straight off, Édouard began to sing in rather a nice voice:

> 'Today is my moment and right now is my story, while I laugh and I cry and I sing . . .
> Today, while all the blossoms still cling to the vine . . .'

And he raised his glass so that Hector would fill it up again.

'You have a really good voice,' said Éléonore with amazement.

> ' . . . I'll taste your strawberries and I'll drink your sweet wine, and a million tomorrows shall all pass away ere I forget all the joy that is mine toooo-daaaay . . .'

Once again, Hector thought to himself that poets were better at getting people to feel things than philosophers were.

'So you could say that the present lasts for ever?' said Édouard after emptying his glass.

'Exactly. That's why you could say that the present is the reflection of eternity in time!'

Hector remembered: that was the last thing Roger had said on the snowmobile!

'It was a Danish philosopher, Kierkegaard, who said that,' said Éléonore. 'He was the first of the existentialists. He thought you had to live life with passion. For him, living was choosing to ride a wild stallion rather than choosing to fall asleep in a hay wagon. I just love him.' Éléonore spoke breathlessly, like a young girl talking about a rock star.

Hector thought that, in fact, Éléonore, with her little plane, lived her life like the rider on a wild stallion. What's more, she'd perhaps considered Hector to be a new stallion, which was flattering in a way.

'He also said that believing in God or getting married must be passionate or personal choices, because there's no rational argument for doing it or not doing it, but that you have to choose, fully committing yourself.'

Hector resolved to read Kierkegaard, because in these two areas, he still hadn't chosen to choose.

Suddenly he also remembered what Noumen had replied to Roger.

'And what was God doing before the world was created?' he asked. 'Was there time then?'

'For St Augustine, no. God created time and space as properties of the universe. For Kant, God gave us time as a way to make sense of the world, in what he called an *a priori* form of intuition, so time is only a reality within our soul. For Leibniz, time isn't within our soul, it's a physical reality outside us, where events follow one another in time, but this reality is created, of course, by God. For these people, before creation there was no time. God was, or rather is, in eternity, which is outside time.'

'And what do physicists say about it? The Big Bang and all that,' asked Édouard.

'Physicists tell us that time doesn't go by everywhere at the same speed,' said Hector, thinking back to his conversation with Hubert about travelling into the future.

'Anyway,' said Édouard, 'at least physicists can do experiments to verify their theories and know whether they're right or wrong. But with philosophy, you can say anything and everything!'

'Yes,' said Éléonore, 'but philosophy teaches you how to think. And then, in the end, you can choose your own little personal philosophy.'

'For example?' asked Hector.

Éléonore looked at him, and Hector wondered if he'd been right to ask the question.

'For example, personally, I've chosen to live only in the present. I certainly never think about the past and I avoid thinking about the future . . . or I just think about the immediate future.'

Éléonore's very blue eyes looked deep into his.

'And how's Hilton these days?' asked Hector.

Éléonore began to laugh.

'Is this another shrink trick? Oh, Hilton's fine, but he's the opposite of me: he lives in the past with his little bubbles, and in the future he wants to start a family.'

Hector thought that Éléonore should have liked Hilton, because he also made passionate and non-rational choices in his life, like drilling holes in the ice in minus fifty degrees, or, tougher still, wanting to start a family with a girl like Éléonore . . . But there you have it: love is often unfair, and Éléonore preferred Hector, who was hardly the king of passionate choices himself.

'How about some champagne to finish?' asked Édouard, because the phrase 'little bubbles' had sparked some memories, which once again just goes to show that the past only exists in the present, and can very quickly go back to being the immediate future, that's to say the future present, if you've been following so far.

HECTOR AND TEMPTATION

After dinner, everyone was quite tired, especially Édouard and Hector. They all decided to go back to their hotel. It was the same hotel that Hector had stayed in the very first time he'd come to this city, when he'd met Ying Li and the old monk. But he'd drunk enough champagne to feel quite merry, and coming back with Édouard and Éléonore saved him from thinking about the past.

They said good night to each other as they got out of the lift, then went back to their rooms, and Hector managed to avoid meeting Éléonore's final gaze in his direction.

When he got into his very comfortable room with its bed that was big enough for at least two people, Hector felt very tired, and he thought to himself that he would have a rest for five minutes before he brushed his teeth, and he lay down fully dressed on the bed.

The conference was still going on, in the same big amphitheatre, but it was very cold and, instead of the lovely navy-blue cushions, everyone was sitting on animal furs.

Above all, Hector noticed everyone had grown awfully old, with bald heads or grey hair, and there were lots of rather cloudy eyes looking at him. He noticed a little old lady who still had a nice smile. It was Marie-Agnès. As for Paul, he looked so old, still and quiet that you almost wondered if he was already dead, but he opened one eye and gave Hector a little nod. Olivier the biologist had grown awfully old too, and yet you could see he was sucking a pickled herring.

Hector counted himself very lucky, first of all because he had on a beautiful Arctic fox fur outfit which was keeping him lovely and warm, and then because even though he had also grown old – he could tell from his wrinkly old hands – he felt fit as a fiddle.

'So, I'm going to talk to you about something that a lot of psychiatrists are interested in and which puts a lot of work their way: the midlife crisis. But I know it's a little late for you.'

There was a murmur from the audience.

'No, it's not too late for us!' shouted Marie-Agnès.

'Absolutely not,' said Olivier, 'we're slap bang in the middle of it!'

And Hector felt a little foolish: he had forgotten that, thanks to medical advances, all these very old people had in fact just reached middle age.

'Well,' he said, 'the midlife crisis is precisely the point when we begin to think about the time we have left, because before, when we're younger, we think about it less, since we live more in the immediate future, and we don't think too much about the limits of our life, even though we know it'll end one day.'

'Does it mean that you're having a midlife crisis when you start measuring your life in dogs?'

Hector recognised Fernand standing in the back row. He had also grown old, but in an even thinner and more upright kind of way. He was holding a big dog on a lead, and Hector recognised Noumen, who hadn't changed one little bit, and was looking at him with his pale and intelligent eyes.

'Yes, measuring your life in dogs,' said Hector, 'that can be a sign. But it's not the only one. A midlife crisis is when you really start to take stock of your life and, above all, when you compare what you expected out of life when you were younger with how it's turned out. Sometimes, things work out well and you end up saying to yourself that you've got what you'd hoped for, or even better.'

'That's what I say to myself, even if it's not easy every day,' said a woman, and Hector recognised Sabine, his patient who thought that life might be a big con. Hector was surprised: Sabine didn't look that much older. She was sitting between her two children, a girl and a boy, who must have been in their twenties and who both looked a little taller than she was.

'Well done,' said Hector. 'But sometimes things don't work out so well, because you don't have what you'd hoped for. Or you do have it, and you're very disappointed. So you tell us that what you hoped for out of life when you were young was the wrong path to take, and you were swayed by your parents and your teachers. And now you want to get off this path! But, of course, it's a little late . . .'

'I also say that to myself from time to time!' said Sabine.

'Ah, that just goes to show that having children doesn't solve everything!' cried Marie-Agnès.

'Nobody said it did,' answered Sabine, sounding a little annoyed.

Suddenly, Hector felt anxious, because he couldn't for the life of him remember if he'd had children with Clara. He began racking his brains to try to remember. And in the meantime he didn't say anything.

'For goodness' sake, Doctor, keep going!' said Marie-Agnès.

'Yes,' said Paul, 'we're wasting time here!'

'Don't forget,' said Olivier, 'our telomeres are getting older.'

But Hector's mind was a complete blank. Had he had children with Clara or not?

Paul began rapping on a pile of programmes resting on his lap, as if to wake Hector up, and it went 'bang, bang, bang' louder and louder.

Somebody was knocking at his bedroom door and Hector went to open it. He already knew who was knocking and he thought to himself that perhaps it would be better not to open it, but he was still half asleep and, by the time he thought that, his body had already opened the door.

'I rang several times,' said Éléonore, 'but since nothing happened I began to get worried, thinking that you'd had a funny turn or something.'

She sat down gracefully in one of the armchairs in the room and lit a cigarette.

'You know tobacco makes you age?'

'Oh, *you*! Of course I know that, but I only have one every now and again . . . or when I'm not quite sure what to say.'

And, again, Hector felt Éléonore's blue eyes lock onto his. Hector felt that his own body, the same one that had opened the door, was beginning to get restless, because he'd sensed Éléonore's body very close to his, a little like two animals that sense each other's presence in the dark.

He thought to himself that it was very difficult to resist temptation when it was put right in front of you. The prayer he used to have to say when he was little was really rather good, since it went: 'Lead us not into temptation'. Perhaps he hadn't said it enough since then!

He tried to think very hard about Clara, but that didn't work all that well because the presence of Éléonore, who was so close and looking at him, was just too much.

Then Hector finally woke up properly; the effects of the champagne had worn off, and suddenly he saw every last detail of the room, which brought back so many memories – even the frosted-glass door of the bathroom, behind which he'd heard a certain someone singing to herself one morning.

And so it was that Hector didn't get up to mischief and he stayed faithful to Clara.

ÉDOUARD IS A GOOD STUDENT

The next day, Hector woke up very early and wasn't in a good mood at all. As he brushed his teeth, he thought that perhaps this was how you knew a good deed was truly good: you didn't necessarily feel better afterwards. He consoled himself with the thought that if he'd given in to temptation he might have been feeling even worse now.

He could have called Clara, but in the end he decided it was better not to, because he was a little annoyed with her. He was a little annoyed with her for not having come with him: with her there, he wouldn't have been led into temptation in the first place. And when temptation came his way, like last night, he had to struggle quite hard to resist it. He knew it wasn't fair to be annoyed with Clara, but he thought it was better to call her later.

As a result of all this, Hector didn't really want to see Éléonore that morning, or Édouard, who had brought her along with him, and he decided that he'd go to the little train station straight away to ask about the old monk. But before that he'd better call Trevor and Katharine.

Because you've realised, of course, that the old Chinese man who was handing out tickets was the old monk. But Hector hadn't recognised him the first time round, because when you're expecting to see someone who always wears an orange robe over one shoulder you don't realise it's them when you see them dressed as a station master. Hector was sure the old monk had recognised him, though, so why hadn't he said anything?

He phoned Trevor and Katharine. Had they heard from the old monk?

'Ah,' said Trevor, 'yes. But we should meet in person to talk about it.'

And he gave Hector their address on the island, a house on one of the slopes of the mountain. They were expecting Hector for breakfast.

As he was leaving the hotel, who do you think Hector bumped into? Édouard!

'I couldn't sleep,' he explained. 'So I went out again.'

Hector preferred not to ask him where he'd been.

So they decided to go and visit Trevor and Katharine together.

And who did Hector and Édouard run into as they waited for their taxi? Éléonore, who was coming back from a little early-morning walk, which had given her rosy cheeks, because in the morning Éléonore's walks were more like runs.

The night before, since Hector didn't want to become another empty glass thrown in Éléonore's face, he'd very gently explained to her why it was better for both of them to go back to their own beds, even if in a parallel world, or indeed a past or future life, things could have turned out differently.

That morning, Éléonore gave Hector a little smile, as if to say that she didn't really have any hard feelings.

And so all three of them decided to go and see Trevor and Katharine together.

Trevor and Katharine were waiting for them in the middle of their garden, which looked a little like a garden from their country, with lots of flowers, and especially some magnificent hydrangeas. In any case, they were the only flowers Hector knew by name.

They went to have breakfast on the veranda, which overlooked the city and the sea in the distance with some islands or patches of distant coastline, and some mountains or clouds – it was hard to tell.

Katharine and Trevor explained that, before, this used to be their home when they lived in the city. Now some friends lived there and lent it to them when they went on holiday.

'Coming back out onto this veranda is like going back in time,' said Katharine.

In fact, thought Hector, if time is a measure of movement, by moving back, you might think you were turning back time, but that wasn't exactly true, since things had kept moving elsewhere, like in your telomeres, for example.

Actually, the tea, the blue and white porcelain, the perfectly done toast and lots of kinds of jam ending in 'berry' all reminded Hector of when he was a little boy and used to go and stay with a family a little like Trevor and Katharine's during the holidays to learn English.

'A view like that . . . it makes me want to go flying,' said Éléonore, looking at the city and the sea in the distance and all the little islands.

'Oh, flying a plane! That's always been a dream of mine,' said Katharine.

Éléonore and Katharine carried on talking. They seemed to get on very well, and it occurred to Hector that when she was young Katharine must have looked a lot like Éléonore. And if that meant that Éléonore would look like Katharine when she was old, she was lucky. Of course, she'd have to find her Trevor between now and then.

What with drinking so much tea, Hector had to go to the toilet. While he was in the house looking for the bathroom, he came across an old black and white photo of Trevor and Katharine, framed and hanging on the wall. They both looked very young and were wearing shorts. Around them was a group of little children who looked so poor that some were almost naked, and they were all staring at the camera with amazement. Behind them was part of a hut which must have been the classroom, and behind that the jungle.

He remembered what Trevor had said about coping with time going by: spend your time changing the things that can be changed.

When he came back, Hector started talking to Trevor about the old monk.

'Hmm, now things get a little tricky,' said Trevor.

And he went off to look for something.

Édouard had fallen asleep in his armchair, but everyone was pretending not to notice.

Trevor came back with a big map and opened it out on the table.

Hector only saw mountains at first, then lakes, and in one corner of the map a border with China.

'It's an old map,' said Trevor, 'because, these days, all this is China too.'

The peaks of the mountains had very beautiful names, like Shishapangma, Gurla Mandhata and Karakal.

Trevor pointed to a valley between three mountains, where there was no city or village name, and nothing was marked on the map. It was right on the border with the country which had become China.

'He was born there,' said Trevor. 'So he wanted to go back there to die.'

Hector had sensed it for a while now, but it came as a bit of a shock to him to realise that the old monk was going to die.

'But how do you get there?'

'By plane,' said Éléonore.

And Hector saw that she'd been looking at the map from the start, and had begun to do some calculations in her head, because even though Éléonore looked at horoscopes she still believed that part of her future present was determined by what she did in the present present.

Just then, Édouard woke up with a start.

'Sorry!' he said, blushing, and seeing everyone looking at him.

Then he turned to Hector.

'I dreamt,' he said, '. . . a distant . . . valley.'

Hector thought that, assuming the Inuit shaman had now come round up there in the camp, he must have been very happy. Unlike a lot of the teachers Hector had given little pills to, the shaman could tell himself that he had at least two good students.

HECTOR AND HISTORY, WHICH
KEEPS REPEATING ITSELF (PART II)

It looked as though a bear was flying the plane, but it was just Éléonore with a big fur hood. It was history repeating itself, Hector thought.

Hector had got to thinking this because he was also drinking some very good champagne from a bottle Édouard had brought – and this time, in a real glass, which showed that things sometimes got better when history repeated itself, contrary to what the philosopher with the enormous moustache liked to think.

What wasn't quite so good, on the other hand, was that instead of flying through the Arctic night (which wasn't that scary, since you couldn't see anything at all outside), this time they were surrounded on all sides by big frightening mountains. Hector and Édouard kept thinking the plane was going to crash into the mountains, taking them with it. But Éléonore always found a way through two big snowy rock faces, because, before they left, she'd studied the map carefully and calculated everything in her head. And she had probably read her horoscope too. Hector remembered that the philosopher with the enormous moustache called this way of living your life 'the Great Style'. And Éléonore had style, no doubt about that.

'The only problem,' she'd said, 'is that I'm not too sure where to land.'

The big problem when you're flying a plane, Éléonore had explained, is that you always have to land eventually. Éléonore always thought of a plane journey in terms of the landing, just as the philosopher with the little moustache thought that our Being-in-the-world was only really worthwhile if we kept thinking that one day it was going to end in death, so our Being-in-the-world was a Being-towards-death, if you follow. But maybe this idea had come to the philosopher when he was just the right age for a midlife crisis. Hector said to himself that he'd check, providing Éléonore managed to land the plane.

Just then, Éléonore looked as if she wanted to fly over a big mountain that was coming towards them, although the big mountain looked too high to fly over. She must have been unable to find a way through, and the plane began to climb with a straining noise that wasn't very reassuring. Édouard quickly poured a last glass of champagne for Hector, and they clinked glasses with their fingers crossed. Suddenly, the plane went into the clouds and they couldn't see anything at all any more and were a lot less scared, but still a little scared. They *knew* the mountain was very close, but they couldn't *feel* it any more.

Éléonore had pushed back her hood, and Hector could see that she didn't look very relaxed either.

Then the cloud seemed to blow away, the plane levelled out again, and, a long way ahead of them, between the clouds, they saw a valley bathed in sunshine.

'There it is!' said Éléonore.

Hector looked at the valley coming towards them, a blanket of soft green in the middle of these vast mountains. He understood why, when you'd known this place once, you might want to come back here to die.

They were getting closer. Hector could see a village and, a little higher up in the foothills of the mountain, a monastery. Then he saw some people watching the plane, a little boy leading a herd of very hairy buffaloes, monks in orange robes coming down from the monastery on a little path, and women in tunics of every colour washing rugs in the river.

Éléonore made a turn, and Hector and Édouard admired the monastery's exquisite architecture, the beauty of the rugs drying in the sun, and the people's kindness as they welcomed them with a big wave. Hector remembered that buffaloes from these parts were called yaks.

Everything was wonderful, but they thought it a little less so when it dawned on them that if Éléonore was going round in circles it wasn't so they could admire the scenery, but because she couldn't see a good spot to land her little plane. Yet it had been fitted both with runners like skis for the snow and little wheels inside which could be lowered.

At the end of the valley, they spotted a lake.

'Damn!' said Éléonore. 'We'd have been better off with a seaplane.'

Well, Hector pointed out, Éléonore really should have thought things through a bit more before they left, and brought a seaplane! But she explained that the lake hadn't been on the map.

'We could try and land on it,' she said. 'It cuts down the risk of a crash landing. But we won't be able to get back . . .'

Hector imagined himself going all the way back on foot surrounded by gigantic mountains. Of course, it was impossible.

So he said to himself, that one way or another, they were all going to end their journey in this valley.

He thought about Clara very hard.

HECTOR AND THE DISTANT VALLEY

ÉLÉONORE spotted a meadow which was more or less flat, right by the lake, and they landed quite smoothly, but it gave the yaks rather a fright and sent them running in every direction.

A little procession came to meet them – people from the village, monks, children, and even one or two rather curious yaks that had retraced their steps and were quite trusting, because, here, people never killed animals.

A young monk spoke English. He explained that this was only the second time in their lives that the people and the yaks had seen an aeroplane. The first time had been the aeroplane which had brought the old monk a week earlier.

'And how did it take off again?' asked Éléonore.

The young monk pointed to the lake, and Hector understood that the plane would never take off ever again. But they'd had time to get the old monk out of it.

They started walking towards the village. The little children kept zigzagging back and forth in front of them, running and laughing as they looked at them, because, while it was the second aeroplane they'd seen, these were the first ever white people. They couldn't get enough of Éléonore's blue eyes. Hector noticed that the children, like their parents, were dressed in all kinds of different tunics made of wool, most probably from yaks. The women were just as lovely as the Inuit, but taller. They had pinker cheeks and lighter-coloured eyes, and they wore pretty necklaces covered in little precious stones. Everyone had wonderful smiles, and yet no one had ever seen a dentist. And there were lots of children, because women were allowed to have as many as they liked, unlike the part of the mountains which had become China.

Hector thought that everyone was always talking about the Mediterranean diet, but that it would probably be a good idea to study the diet here, especially since by the time he reached the village, he felt very tired from the little walk. But the children, who must have run twice that distance as they zigzagged back and forth in front of them, didn't seem tired at all, unlike Édouard, who wanted to sit down right away and if possible have a drink. The young monk said they could have something to drink at the monastery, but that they'd better hurry if they wanted to see the old monk. No time to go sightseeing in the village with its stone-tiled houses or have a conversation with these charming people. They had to climb a steep little path covered with stones which led up to the monastery. Hector and Édouard were out of breath, but Éléonore wasn't at all.

'It's the altitude,' she said. 'You're not used to it.'

'We're fine,' said Édouard, because admitting that he wasn't as strong as a girl always annoyed him.

In the monastery, they went through several rooms whose walls were covered with very old paintings on wood which depicted devils with huge fangs fighting with very beautiful gods wearing earrings, and also normal people, and sometimes monkeys. It was a lot more complicated than it sounds, but, as the old monk was waiting, they didn't have time to look, and we don't have time to explain it to you either.

They also went past some squatting monks who were chanting, but they didn't look at all surprised to see Hector, Édouard and Éléonore.

Then the young monk stopped in front of a very old carved wooden door, and on it there was a crowned figure balancing on one foot inside a big circle, as if it was playing with a hoop.

The young monk knocked, and another fatter, not so young monk answered the door.

Édouard and Éléonore motioned to Hector that they'd rather let him go in by himself.

Hector went through.

In a very bare little room, lying on his side with his head resting on a pillow, the old monk was looking at him, smiling.

HECTOR, THE OLD MONK AND TIME

'YOU see,' said the old monk, 'when people started talking about how old I was, I thought I'd better make myself scarce.'

Hector didn't say anything, because he wanted to let the old monk do all the talking, since it seemed to Hector that he didn't have much time left, not in this world anyway.

'All these people . . .' said the old monk. 'All these poor people who are scared of dying. I'm a sort of symbol, you see. So I said to myself that when they found out how old I was lots of people were going to flock to my religion, as if that would bring them longevity.'

Hector thought then of all the people in his country who desperately wanted to add years to their lives and have their midlife crisis as late as possible. Some already practised little bits of the monk's religion, for the same reason as they'd gone on the Mediterranean diet: to get old less quickly.

'Wanting to stay young or live for a long time would be the worst reason to join us,' said the old monk.

He reminded Hector that attachment to earthly life was a very big obstacle in both his religion and Hector's, and in almost all other religions too.

Hector didn't say anything to that either, because he wasn't a great believer himself and didn't practise his religion. Even in front of a monk from another religion, he would have felt a little embarrassed saying so. (Some people will tell you that the old monk's religion is not a religion, and we could discuss it till the cows come home, but defining things doesn't get you very far, as Pascal, the philosopher Hector liked, once said.)

Even so, in the end, Hector asked the old monk if this business about his age was true.

'Oh,' said the old monk, 'what does it matter in the end? How do you like the tea? Here, they add butter and barley.'

But the old monk could tell that Hector, even though he didn't dare ask the question, would have really liked to know.

'Well, as I've always looked young for my age, it was quite easy to arrange – the story of a father who disappears and a long-lost son who comes back – at a time when there weren't a lot of photos and no TV yet, and when I had to travel around quite a lot. It gave me some freedom for a few years . . . I had time to arrange quite a lot of things.'

The old monk coughed, and it took him a while to catch his breath. Hector wished he could have done something, but he knew there wasn't much he could do. The old monk wouldn't have wanted machines blinking away all around him.

'Anyway, all that was necessary,' said the old monk.

Hector found it interesting to see that the old monk

had also been a man of action, like Trevor and the Roman general. Unlike those people who believed it was good to 'let go', leave everything behind and spend lots of time in search of inner peace without ever getting out of their chairs again. Even compassion for your enemies, yet another teaching you also found in Hector's religion, shouldn't stop you from trying to stand in the way of what your enemies were doing, and even putting quite a lot of effort into it. But Hector could see all too well that the time for action was over for the old monk.

'And being a station master . . . did you like it?' asked Hector, just so he'd feel less sad.

'Oh, yes! For a start, it's the best way to hide, you know, being in plain sight. Even you didn't recognise me! Or Trevor and Katharine either, my dear friends! But I didn't say anything when I saw you, because the place was being watched very closely, and I was sure that we'd see each other again . . .'

Hector offered the old monk a little tea, and he took a mouthful.

'And I'd spent so many years cut off from the world, in this monastery, and before, of course . . .'

Hector remembered that, before, the old monk had spent many years in various places where they'd wanted to force him to think the right way. To do that, they'd locked him up for a very long time by himself, all alone. But the old monk wasn't thinking about all those years spent facing a wall any more; he was smiling as he told Hector his memories of being a station master.

'How the world has changed! Especially the women from your part of the world! Everyone travels a lot more than before. At the same time, I felt that most people don't know what they're looking for. I realised that, for many people in the world, life had become a lot more entertaining than before, and they could arrange their lives as a continuous upsurge of novelty, as one of your philosophers said. All these trips, changing jobs several times in their life, and new loves too. I understand that people have become slaves to this desire for continuous renewal and improvement. But growing old, leaving this life and this world full of promise, then becomes more difficult to accept than if you live in the countryside in a very harsh environment that hardly changes over the course of your lifetime. But now . . . You're going to have a lot of work!' said the old monk, with the little laugh Hector was so fond of.

A little later on, Édouard and Éléonore came in, and the old monk told Éléonore that she looked very like Katharine when she was her age.

Éléonore blushed, and then afterwards she asked the old monk if he thought the present and eternity were the same. And the old monk said, of course, the present was also eternity and, at the same time, it was nothingness, since it dissolved at the same time as it existed.

'The present is eternity, nothingness and at the same time everything that exists,' said the old monk, 'because nothing exists outside the present. And, of course, this everything is really the Whole of everything, so it's also you and me, and even the clouds and the yaks and the mountains outside . . .' He closed his eyes, as he was very tired.

Hector, Édouard and Éléonore exchanged glances to let each other know it was time to go.

But the old monk opened his eyes and looked at Édouard.

'Dear Édouard,' he said. 'The Kablunak-who-counts-fast! Would you like to know exactly how old I am?'

Édouard said that he'd rather not know exactly, but that he'd really like to know how the old monk had stayed young for so long.

'Good genes,' said the old monk, smiling.

Then he closed his eyes, and fell asleep.

HECTOR AND ETERNITY

Hector went back to see the old monk once more during the day. And once the following morning. The third time, the young monk told him there was no point any more.

Of course, there was going to be a ceremony with all the monks and the people from the village, and even the yaks, who were part of the Great Whole. Hector would really have liked to stay, but Éléonore said that with the clouds she could see coming, if they didn't leave straight away, she couldn't say when they'd be able to, perhaps not even until spring.

Since Hector wanted to avoid spending long weeks having talks with Éléonore about time and eternity surrounded by yaks – because he knew that no matter how hard he tried he wouldn't have been able to stick to the Right View or the Right Action, and the whole thing would have ended up under a yak-wool blanket – he said okay to leaving straight away.

He went off to look for Édouard. In fact, Édouard had had time to discover the local drink, a kind of fermented yak's milk, and he'd made some new friends among the men in the village, who had also learnt to say 'Jourgoodhel'. The single young women found Édouard very funny, as Hector could clearly see when he arrived at lunchtime.

Édouard said that he was going to stay in the valley.

'Are you mad?' said Hector. 'What about the Inuit?'

Édouard explained that the Inuit didn't need him any more. Now, they were able to run their buying and selling operation all by themselves. In any case, he would return on the next plane that came through there and, since Édouard would mark out a proper runway, it wouldn't land in the lake. But, even so, Hector didn't understand why Édouard wanted to stay.

'It's this constant need for novelty,' said Édouard. 'But I think that being here may be the way to finally leave that behind.'

'Do you want to become a monk?'

'Definitely not,' said Édouard. 'I don't think I'm cut out for it! I just want to change a little. And also, this place,' – he gestured towards the vast mountains, the monks coming down the steep little path and the yaks roaming peacefully – 'it helps you to really get in touch with time, eternity and all that.'

Hector thought that Édouard had given some quite good reasons. He could always come back and get him with Éléonore after winter.

As he walked to the plane, he took the time to write in his little notebook:

Time Exercise with no number: Try to experience the present as eternity and feel that it's everything and nothing at the same time.

Hector knew this exercise was difficult, but, with a little bit of practice every day, you could get there now and again. That might make people feel more comfortable with time going by. He joined Éléonore, who seemed very happy. She had spotted a little meadow for taking off — actually quite a short incline, Hector noticed, and just past it a ravine which he'd rather not see the bottom of.

'Of course, as we drop, we'll get our speed up. After that, we should be fine.'

When the plane began to drop, Hector had to think very hard about the old monk, who said that attachment to earthly life was a very big obstacle, and those seconds seemed to last a very long time. Then Éléonore pulled the plane up and they took to the skies again over the big mountains bathed in golden sunlight.

And Hector looked at them for a long time, those big mountains.

By telling himself that they too only existed in the present, for a brief moment Hector experienced eternity.

HECTOR RETURNS

WHEN Hector met up with old François again, he
asked him what he'd thought of all the philosophers he'd had time to read or reread.

'They make you think,' said old François.

Hector remembered that Éléonore had said the same
thing.

'François? Are you there?'

And a lady opened the office door and popped her
head round it. From the look of old François, Hector
understood what had made him so happy. As, for once,
the lady was around the same age as the mothers of the
young women François usually fell for, Hector thought
that this old-fashioned romance stood a good chance of
becoming the future present. Hector wondered whether
old François had managed to change the way he loved by
reading philosophy – if so, it was worth going back to.

Hector met up with his patients again, and some were
even beginning to get impatient waiting for him to come
back. For them, time had gone by very slowly.

Roger told Hector that he'd seen him on TV.

'I didn't know you were going to see monks,' said
Roger.

'They're not quite the same sort of monks as in our religion,' said Hector.

'Perhaps they are!' said Roger.

And he told Hector that in the past some people had thought that the founder of Hector and Roger's religion and that of the old monk's were actually the same person who had come to visit this world at two different times and in two different places. Each time, the local people who lived in these two places quite far away from each other had told the story of his time on earth in their own way. They had also mixed it in with their local religions.

'The lessons taught both times were compassion for all beings, even for your enemies, non-attachment to worldly possessions, the idea of an end of time,' said Roger, obviously very much in his element.

Hector wasn't too sure what to make of it, but he promised himself he'd do some proper reading, when he had time.

After which, Roger told him that he was determined to stop all his medication and Hector had to run late for all his other sessions that day.

Later on, Hector saw Hubert. Hector saw straight away that he was very happy.

'I was right, Doctor, to keep believing in our love! In fact, she's like a comet – she left, but she came back!'

Hector thought to himself that if you took this comet metaphor further, this would mean that Hubert's wife would leave again one day, but he didn't say that. He wanted Hubert to enjoy the present and perhaps manage to bring about a better present in the future.

Fernand hadn't changed a bit. Only, now, he had two dogs. Hector was a little shaken when he saw that the new dog was the same breed as Noumen. It could almost have been his twin, with the same pale eyes which never left Hector for a second.

'In a way, this means I can double the years I have left in dog lives,' said Fernand with a funny little cawing sound.

Hector realised that this was Fernand's laugh. It was the first time he'd heard it. Perhaps Fernand was going to make some new friends.

Little Hector said that he was less bored in class.

'Why?' asked Hector.

'I've got a friend,' said Little Hector. 'Me and her swap notes in class.'

Hector could tell that Little Hector was very proud of swapping notes with a little girl his age. And what about school? you say. All right, but to be happy in life, isn't learning very early on how to talk to girls and understand them at least as important as doing well at school?

Sabine seemed more relaxed than last time.

'I decided to go part time,' she said. 'There's a lot less pressure and more time for the children. Of course, it's not great for my career. But my husband says he couldn't care less.'

Hector's wish for Sabine was that her husband would always feel that way, and he thought to himself that truly, in life, it was always the women who took the most risks.

Hector also thought to himself that all these people were doing better since he'd gone on his trip. So that proved he could do it again. He also saw Marie-Agnès again.

'Actually, after you left, I dumped Paul.'

'But why?' asked Hector.

He didn't understand – Paul and Marie-Agnès seemed to get on so well.

'We were caught up in the same madness,' said Marie-Agnès. 'Always more, do you know what I mean?'

Hector knew very well.

'I don't want to change,' said Marie-Agnès. 'I want to stay young for as long as possible. But I'd like to be with a man who doesn't care about that at all. An intellectual type excited by his work who couldn't give two hoots about going grey or getting a pot belly, well, not too much of one, anyway. Or else, a greying cowboy type who thinks about his horses . . .'

Hector said to himself that he'd see to it that Hubert and Marie-Agnès found themselves waiting together in the waiting room one day, when the comet had left again.

HECTOR AND CLARA AND . . .

THE doctor, who was in fact a friend of Hector's, told him that the baby-to-be looked in fine fettle. Hector looked at the photo taken inside Clara's tummy and said to himself that this definitely proved that time wasn't a human creation, since it would take time for the baby to get bigger and become aware of time going by. And – why not – even take up German and decide to write philosophy books about time.

'It's incredible – I'd swear the baby looks like you.'

Hector said excuse him, but *he* didn't see why that was incredible.

'No, no,' said Clara, 'I meant that the baby looks like you, already!'

Hector knew that at other times the baby would look more like Clara, then like him again, and then one day this little person would still be young when he and Clara no longer were.

He also thought to himself that he'd forgotten to write down a very important time exercise.

Hector took out his little notebook and made a note.

Clara looked over his shoulder and burst out laughing.

Eternity, thought Hector, let this moment right here become eternity.

HECTOR IN THE GARDEN

HECTOR was walking in a garden. The sky was a deep blue, with little white clouds perfectly lined up all around like on a pretty tapestry.

He followed a path edged with giant hydrangeas, and other flowers whose names he didn't know. In the distance, he saw someone walking towards him. It was the old monk.

The old monk was holding something in his hand, and Hector realised it was his own notebook! Even though he knew that the old monk always had a nice way of putting things, Hector was still a bit worried about hearing what he thought of his little exercises.

They both started walking together, and Hector was careful not to walk too fast.

Somehow Hector just knew that the garden had no boundaries. In the distance, he could see people strolling along other paths or resting in the shade.

'Where are we?' asked Hector.

'In a place from your religion,' said the old monk.

'But in my dream too,' said Hector.

'Who knows?' said the old monk. 'By the way, I read

your time exercises. They're interesting. You've come a long way.'

'Thank you,' said Hector. 'But I feel as if I haven't got to the big picture.'

'That's to be expected,' said the old monk. 'You're still so young . . .'

They both sat down on a stone bench in the shade of a giant hydrangea.

'There are two levels,' said the old monk.

Hector was very happy, as he had a feeling that the old monk was going to tell him some important things.

'The first level,' said the old monk, 'is what you practise in your civilisation back home. It all comes down to organising your time better, not wasting time and, of course, doing everything you can to stay young for as long as possible. You have hundreds of books to help you.'

'Are they helpful?' asked Hector.

The old monk gave the little laugh Hector was so fond of.

'Until you manage to get past that level, you might as well do it the best you can,' said the old monk.

Hector said to himself that Paul, Marie-Agnès and lots of others would be glad to know that the old monk didn't think their efforts were ridiculous.

'Of course,' said the old monk, 'it doesn't necessarily prepare you for growing old and dying, which you can't avoid anyway.'

'What about the second level?' asked Hector.

The old monk smiled.

'Do you remember your last exercise? Experience the present as eternity. Because it's always today for us.'

'Yes,' said Hector.

'That's a way in,' said the old monk. 'But it's not for everyone . . .'

That was something Hector loved about the old monk: he didn't want to force anyone to see things the way he did.

'. . . and also, by wanting detachment at all costs, you can end up getting too attached to detachment . . .'

That reminded Hector of what he'd said to Éléonore about wanting to try to run away from time, which in itself became another prison.

'So?' said Hector.

'I really liked that saying about changing the things that can be changed, accepting the things that can't and knowing the difference.'

'It's not mine,' said Hector.

'Yes, I know, but it's a very good exercise. To be done every day. Detachment, but not inaction.'

Detachment, but not inaction! said Hector to himself. Here was an excellent motto to round off his little exercises.

'But that's not all,' said the old monk.

Blast, thought Hector, he still didn't have his conclusion for coping with the passage of time.

'So?' asked Hector.

The old monk smiled.

'You need to think it over a little more, my dear friend. Take action, all right, but why? Why not do nothing?'

Hector didn't know the answer.

'Well, time to go – see you around, I'm sure,' said the old monk.

And the old monk went calmly on his way. Hector saw that he'd left his little notebook on the bench. Hector picked it up and wrote:

Detachment, but not inaction.

As the old monk had suggested, he kept thinking it over.

Take action, but why?

He began to think about Édouard. He'd become less impatient by working with the Inuit. Then he thought of the photo of Trevor and Katharine surrounded by little children in the jungle. He remembered Éléonore, always happy to take people places in her plane. And Ying Li too, who looked so happy watching her little boy, or seeing her mother and her sisters in a nice house.

'The second level! I've got it!' he shouted.

'Are you talking in your sleep now?' said Clara.

Later, Hector realised that he'd forgotten the end of his dream. He couldn't remember the idea that had made him shout 'I've got it!' any more.

But if you've read this book properly, you'll already have guessed.

AUTHOR'S ACKNOWLEDGEMENTS

I am grateful to my father and Hélène for listening and offering advice.

Thanks also to my friends from the two deltas, with whom it is always a pleasure to spend time.

Not forgetting, of course, Odile Jacob, Bernard Gotlieb and their teams for all their hard work on this latest instalment of Hector's adventures.

When authors are asked to explain what made them write their books or come up with a new character, they always want to give worthy reasons. Voltaire might have said he wrote *Candide* to criticise the Ancien Régime, religious intolerance, Leibniz and utopian ideals in an amusing and entertaining fashion. All of which would be true, but you need only read the book to understand why Voltaire really created Candide: he had fun writing about his adventures! Much more than he must have done working on his epic poems and tragedies, which have become tedious for modern readers, and were no doubt already tedious at the time, to the extent that I wonder if Voltaire himself was not bored writing them.

If you were to ask me why I created Hector and his adventures, I might reply that I wanted to tackle psychological and philosophical themes in an entertaining way; to revive the French tradition of philosophical *contes*, or fables; to both move and enrich my readers, and so on.

None of this would be untrue exactly, but as a psychiatrist I am generally suspicious of people giving me good reasons for having behaved in one way or another, so I ask them to tell me about the circumstances leading up to their actions.

These were the circumstances: it was winter and I had

gone along on a trip to Hong Kong with an art dealer friend of mine (I am not very good at holidays, so I always try to accompany friends who have a purpose). I was meant to be writing a serious book on happiness for my French publisher (my own idea, no less), but every time I sat at my computer and wrote a few lines, I was overwhelmed with indescribable boredom. This book on happiness was making me unhappy. On top of that, I was going through a period of questioning and doubt – Was I really going to carry on practising psychiatry until I could no longer get out of my chair? Would I still be a roving bachelor when the only women interested in me had serious unresolved father issues, if not grandfather issues? My friend sensed something was up and tried to cheer me up by showing me the highlights of the city-state by night, but it was no use.

Then one morning while brushing my teeth in a freezing-cold bathroom – a remnant of the British colonial era? – Hector was born! I could picture him clearly, younger than me, somewhat naive, full of good intentions – I have a few of those myself – and trying his best to understand the world and help his patients. I knew straight away that telling the story of Hector's journeys would be a joy, that I would not have to hold his hand but rather it would be him carrying me along on his adventures, drawing of course on my own experiences and those of my patients, as well as dreams and books I had read.

As for the form it took, the *conte*, I would not dare compare myself to Voltaire, but many readers of the Hector series have urged me to re-read *Candide*. Doing so alerted me to the deep impression it must have made on me as a boy, and the extent to which it continues to influence me to this day.

So thank you to Voltaire and Hong Kong, Hector's 'parents', and to my readers, who have encouraged me in letting me know I am not the only one entertained by Hector.

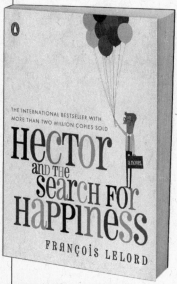

Hector and the Secrets of Love

ISBN 978-0-14-311947-0

Having found that love seems virtually inseparable from happiness, Hector begins taking notes on this powerful emotion. But unbeknownst to him, Clara, the doctor's beloved, is making her own investigations into love. As much a love story as a novel about love, *Hector and the Secrets of Love* is a feel-good life manual wrapped in a globe-trotting adventure, told with the blend of a fairy tale's naive wisdom and a satirist's dry wit that has won Hector fans around the world.

PENGUIN
BOOKS